THE DRAGON KINGS

ASPEN

BOOK 2

KIMBERLY LOTH

Cover design by Rebecca Frank

Interior design by Colleen Sheehan
Write Dream Repeat Book Design LLC

For
Grandma and Grandpa Klungle
Grandma and Grandpa Loth
Grandma and Grandpa DeVito
Thanks for making my childhood magical

CHAPTER 1

S NOW STARTED TO fall as Sid drove into the parking lot. He supposed it was appropriate. He always loved winter because the snow covered the ground in a blanket of white—a beauty he looked forward to every year. Maybe this year it would cover the stain of the deaths that seemed to plague him.

Snow clung to his hair as he walked toward the church. A church he didn't want to enter. Sid knew he should feel sad or angry, but mostly he was numb, and his mind was blank. He didn't know what to think. Over the past few months, everything he knew about his own race, the dragons, was flipped on its end when one of them had started eating people.

Sid was tired of funerals. He thought for sure after they got Marcellus, he wouldn't have to attend another one of these. But people were dying. People he cared about. He wondered when the deaths would end. His heart hurt.

Tori caught him when he walked in. She wrapped her arms around his neck and sobbed into his shoulder.

"I can't believe she's dead."

"Neither can I," he said and patted the back of her head. He wasn't quite sure how to comfort her. They weren't even friends. Or they hadn't been since he and Aspen started dating. Tori pulled away a few seconds later and brought a tissue up to her nose.

"I was such a brat to her."

"You weren't that bad."

"Yeah, I was." She sniffed and lowered her eyes. "Do you think they found anything on her camera?"

Sid shrugged. He knew what was on the camera, but the police hadn't released the details on that yet, and he wasn't about to tell the biggest gossip in the school.

Tori squeezed his hand and gave him a small smile before she went and sat with her family. Sid spotted Aspen's parents and Rowan. They'd saved him a seat.

He sat next to Rowan, who was red-eyed but not crying. Sid was never terribly comfortable with Rowan because Aspen's brother always felt so much fear. When Sid was around him, he had to consciously shut off his gift of taking on emotions. Though today, Sid had enough sadness of his own that he shut off his gift before he even entered the church. He didn't want to add everyone else's on top of his own.

Aspen's parents stared straight ahead, almost as if they were in shock. Sid took a minute to reflect on all that had happened over the last few days. It was strange to think that Halloween was only three days ago. That stupid party where Marc found Aspen, and Sid did something he never thought he'd do. He killed one of his own. His stomach lurched as he thought of it, even though he'd done the right thing. He swallowed a few times. Marcellus was a monster. They couldn't allow him to live.

But it was the first time Sid had killed anyone. If he lived and reigned as king, he'd have to do it again, but he didn't know if he could. As king, he'd have to pass judgment over dragons who broke the law.

Most kings only had to exercise that power three or four times during their kingships, but that was three or four more times than he wanted to. Maybe the best thing to do would be to turn himself in and let the council dole out his own punishment.

Everyone quieted when the service started. Sid couldn't watch as the reverend droned on for a while about what a good person she was, how she loved life and was so passionate. Sid agreed with all those things, though he might have added a few. Like her sharp eye and love for those around her even though she didn't let on how much she cared. It was obvious the reverend had never spoken to her before she died.

A group of senior girls sang a song about dying too young. After that, they opened the service up to those who wanted to say nice things about her. Sid felt like he should get up and say something but found he didn't have the words. He hadn't known her nearly as long as everyone else had. He felt like a fraud even being at the funeral.

As the reverend got up to close the service, Aspen slid into the seat next to him, eyes blazing and hair flying in a million different directions. She took his breath away like she always did.

Sid raised his eyebrows at her. "Isn't it a little rude to come late to a funeral?"

Aspen shrugged and looked away from him as she spoke. "She's dead. It's not like she cares. Besides, I was taking care of more important things."

Sid looked down at her. "You could've waited. This is Mrs. Dufour's funeral." People around them started to get up and leave. Sid wasn't about to let Aspen off the hook. Mrs. Dufour was her favorite teacher. He still wasn't sure why she would show up so late.

Aspen crossed her arms, looked up at him, and huffed. "No. I couldn't have. The media is releasing the photos this afternoon. I needed to make sure they spun it right. It has to be absolutely clear that there is no longer a dragon out there killing people. Between the pictures Mrs. Dufour had on her camera and the ones I got of you, uh, beheading Marcellus, we can show that the dragons took care of the problem themselves."

Sid put his arm along the bench and pulled her close. "Why do you care so much, huh? We have resources, you know. The problem will fix itself." He was pretty sure Aspen was lying to him. She had taken care of the media yesterday and had no reason to go this morning.

Aspen shrugged. "I don't want to leave it to chance." She shimmied out of his embrace. "She was the only teacher that actually liked me." Aspen looked away from him. Her shoulders trembled, and her hands shook as she brushed her hair out of her eyes. She may not admit it, but this death affected her more than the others. Maybe she couldn't handle this funeral. Sid had learned in the last few months that everyone dealt with grief differently.

Sid turned her face so she was looking at him. "It's okay to be sad."

"We were so close to ending the deaths. If she'd just waited a day to go out and take pictures, or if we'd caught him twenty-four hours earlier, she wouldn't be dead."

"You can't play the what-if game. Marcellus killed her, and now he's dead. He can't kill anyone else. That's something we should celebrate."

Sid had been certain there wouldn't be any more deaths. But park rangers discovered Mrs. Dufour's camera the day after Sid killed Marcellus. Aspen's dad had the camera. It had been set up on a timer to take automatic photos and captured the teacher's death. It also put her time of death at two in the afternoon, and Sid killed Marcellus around midnight.

When Aspen's parents found out she had been wandering around at night taking pictures of a murderous dragon, they were pretty pissed off. Ultimately, they accepted that the dragon responsible for the deaths was dead. The media was a little harder to convince.

Aspen fiddled with the edge of her coat. "She was always so supportive. She didn't like dragons, but she always told me if she spotted them when she was out with the wolves. Now she's dead. The pictures show she knew exactly what Marc was going to do. She must've been so scared." Aspen's voice cracked, and Sid pulled her close.

"I know. I'm sorry."

She sobbed into his chest. He'd never seen her this upset before. He didn't know how to handle it except to continue to hold her. After a few minutes, she pulled away and sniffed. He grabbed a tissue out of the box sitting on the pew and handed it to her. She took it, blew her nose, and straightened her shoulders.

"It's time to go. The news will be on soon, and we need to make sure that they report Mrs. Dufour's death as taking place before you killed Marcellus. We can't let the government get involved."

Sid nodded and took her hand. He pulled her out of the little church where they'd attended so many funerals in the last three months. He hoped he wouldn't have to come back here. Ever.

CHAPTER 2

A SPEN AND SID went back to Sid's house after the funeral to watch the news. Aspen didn't spend all morning hassling news reporters just to have them change the story. She refused to give them her pictures unless they promised to spin the story the right way, and they were desperate for her pictures. No one had ever taken a picture of dragons fighting among themselves.

Aspen should've been on time to the funeral, but she'd been too close to Mrs. Dufour to sit through the whole thing. It felt as if she'd burst open and say something she'd regret. The ache of loss had settled deep in her chest. She wanted to rip it out and not feel anything, but didn't know how.

Theo was waiting in the theater room watching a horror flick. He was addicted to those things.

"Hey, dude, how was the funeral?"

"Awful," Sid replied, flinging himself down on the couch. "They all are."

"How long until the news conference?"

Sid looked at the clock and waved Aspen over. "Fifteen minutes." Aspen sank onto the couch next to him and curled into him. He held her tight.

Theo flicked the movie off and disappeared. He came back a couple of minutes later with a bowl of popcorn, picked up the remote, and switched over the screen to the television. It was already on channel four, but Theo muted the sound.

"So, Aspen, what does it take to frighten you?" Theo asked.

Aspen unfolded herself from Sid and grabbed a handful of popcorn. "Not much, why?"

"Did you tell Sid about your own scare with a golden dragon?"

Aspen snapped her eyes up. She hadn't told Sid about what happened after he left on Halloween night. She didn't want him to worry. But as she was taking pictures of Marc's ashes, a massive dragon flew right at her. She figured he was a relative of Marc's who was grieving. Though she couldn't imagine anyone mourning that sleazy bastard.

"What scare?" Sid asked, sitting down next to her.

"It was nothing. How do you know about that?" Aspen asked Theo.

He gave her a wicked smile. "Because I wanted to see if I could scare you. I've never felt one ounce of fear from you. Why is that?"

"Wait, that was you?" Aspen had been around enough dragons to know they all had distinct appearances. Some had longer snouts or wider bodies. Some had big spikes on their tails, and others did not. But Marc and Theo looked almost identical in dragon form. That's actually why she thought the dragon was a relative.

Theo didn't answer. He just threw more popcorn into his mouth. Aspen didn't want to admit it, but he'd scared the snot out of her. Her fear just hadn't set in until he left. She'd never felt like she was in danger around any dragons until that moment.

Sid placed two fingers on Aspen's chin and turned her so she was facing him. "What's he talking about?"

Aspen sighed. "After you disintegrated Marc, I went to take pictures of the ashes, and this huge dragon flew right at me. For a second

I thought he was going to eat me, but he veered off at the last minute and flew away. I didn't know it was Theo."

Sid glared at Theo. "Why'd you do that?"

"I already told you. I wanted to see if I could scare her. Turns out I can't." He dropped a piece of popcorn on the black leather and flicked it off onto the floor.

"Why—" Sid began.

"What the hell is she doing here?" Sid's sister, Pearl, stood by the door with her hands on her hips and eyes narrowed. Her dark red hair had been pulled back into a bun, giving her a severe look. Anyone would be scared of her. Except Aspen.

"She's—" Sid started again.

"I'm Sid's girlfriend, and the sooner you get used to that idea, the easier all of our lives will be. I'm not going anywhere." Aspen wasn't in the mood to deal with any drama. After what happened at the party, she wasn't going to let anyone tell her what to do. "I think I like you better as a dragon."

Pearl sank down on the ottoman in front of Sid. "Tell me you didn't tell her about us." Her lips were pressed in a tight line, but her eyes betrayed her worry.

"She figured it out on her own," Sid said.

That wasn't entirely true. Aspen figured it out on her own, but only after a lot of help from Sid. Apparently, Sid was scared of his sister, even if Aspen was not. But Aspen kept her mouth shut because she knew if she let them talk, she'd learn things she didn't already know.

"How much does she know?" Pearl asked, fiddling with her bun until her hair fell into waves on her shoulders. Every dragon Aspen had met as a human was stunning. She wondered if they got to choose their human forms. The more she found out about the dragon world, the more she realized how little she knew about them.

Sid grabbed a handful of popcorn. "I don't know. A lot." He shoved the whole handful in his mouth. He wouldn't be saying anything for a several seconds.

Pearl rolled her eyes at Sid and faced Aspen. "Do you know who he is?"

"You mean that he's the king?"

Pearl sucked in a breath and nodded her head. She glowered at Sid. "I can't believe you told her that. What if she's a spy for the arctic dragons? Seriously, do you ever think with your head around this girl?"

Sid shrugged and tried to smile, but it looked quite comical with his cheeks stuffed with popcorn. Aspen snorted.

Pearl tapped her finger against her lips for a few seconds and then spoke again.

"Did you know he's in love with you?"

"Yeah. So?" Aspen remembered vague conversations with Sid about how if Pearl found out about the tattoos, he'd be in big trouble. Sid tried to explain the significance of the marks to her, but she was still foggy on the details. All she knew was they had to be kept secret.

Sid's eyes went big. He chewed quickly. Aspen's eyes darted between the two siblings. Sid shook his head at Pearl, and she gave him a grin and turned back to Aspen.

"Did he tell you that by being in love with you, he's basically sentenced himself to death?"

Sid shook his head again and tried to speak, but he choked on a piece of popcorn and began coughing. Both girls ignored him.

Aspen didn't know how to respond.

"I didn't know that." Aspen looked at her hands. Marc told her something like that, but she thought he was just messing with her, playing on her fear. So much had happened that night, and she'd forgotten about what he said.

Pearl stood up and paced in front of the couch. "As long as no one else finds out, he's okay, but if you were to ever love him back, his life would be over. Because it would be impossible to keep that a secret."

"What?" Aspen was confused.

"Dragons mate for life. They only fall in love once. Fortunately, there is a safeguard in place if that love goes unrequited. If you two stay away from each other, his love for you will fade, and he'll able to love his queen. But if you fall in love with him, he won't be able to take a queen, and the council will kill him."

Aspen let out a breath. "Why?" She was already in love with him.

"Because Sid needs a strong queen. The dragons won't let him lead without one."

Aspen's mind spun. Sid's death sentence was already written in stone. As soon as Pearl or anyone else found out, he'd be killed. Her pulse began to race, and her palms went clammy.

Sid finally stopped coughing. "Pearl, you've said enough. I think you should let me finish explaining this to her."

Pearl spun to face him. "Obviously, you've been leaving out crucial details. She had no idea what she was doing to you."

Theo laughed out loud, and everyone's heads turned to look at him.

"What's so funny?" Pearl asked, rolling her eyes at him.

"A fully grown dragon chasing her with its mouth wide open, and she doesn't feel an ounce of fear, but the idea of Sid dying scares her to death."

Pearl looked back and forth between Aspen and Sid. "You really care about him, don't you?" she finally asked.

Aspen looked down at her hands again. "I do. Obviously, I'm not in love with him, but we've grown pretty close." She hoped her lie was convincing to Pearl. She now understood why the tattoos had to be kept secret.

Pearl stood up. "I've waited long enough. This ends. Now. Enjoy your last days together because when I come back, you're not allowed to see each other anymore."

She fled from the room before anyone else could say anything. No one moved for a full thirty seconds. Aspen's mind was racing with the implications.

"Sid is that true? If I fall in love with you, will they kill you?" She couldn't let Theo know the truth. Aspen wished they were alone.

Sid shrugged and reached for her. She scooted away.

"I can't believe you never told me that."

She crossed her arms and fumed. It wouldn't have made any difference. She'd fallen in love with him first, but he still could've told her. She could've stayed away from him. But she shook her head, knowing that would've been impossible. Was there really anything she could've done?

The news started, and all conversation died. To Aspen's relief, the story was just as they told her it would be. They watched the rest and the talk show that came on after it, which analyzed the deaths. People were still suspicious of the dragons, but no one was calling for nuking their nests, so Aspen figured it could be a lot worse.

After they turned the TV off, Aspen wanted to talk about everything, but Theo was still in the room, so she asked something else that had been bugging her.

"You said I didn't have to worry about the news getting my story right because the dragons would take care of that. What did you mean?"

"When the humans became the dominant race on Earth, we had to figure out how to work with them. At first, dragons befriended humans like I did with you, communicating only with our minds, but after the dragon wars, we needed a more efficient mode. Especially because the human population had exploded. We learned how to take on human forms. Now we have ambassadors living as humans in Washington, DC and other major cities around the world. The government recognizes us just as they would any foreign government. Over the last several decades, the king has even gone to meet with the president a few times."

Aspen gaped at him. "I want to meet the president."

"Trust me, you don't. We only meet with her when things are bad. If we hadn't caught Marcellus, we would've had to. It's not usually a happy meeting."

Aspen chewed on that information. "Do you think I could be one of those ambassadors?"

"You're not a dragon."

"So? I'm engrained pretty deeply into your world." More so than anyone knew. She hated having to be cryptic. Maybe Theo would leave soon.

Sid shrugged. "I know, but it's not quite what you think it is. Let's worry about that later."

She felt like Sid was leaving out some pretty important details. He was being intentionally vague. She wanted to believe it was because Theo was in the room, but she had a feeling he was intentionally hiding things he didn't want her to know. She thought of how she could argue with Theo in the room. She opened her mouth to try, but Ella burst in.

"You won. Those newsmen didn't stand a chance against you," she exclaimed and plopped herself down next to Aspen. "This calls for a celebration. We should all head to Bozeman, do dinner, and catch a movie." Ella, her boss and friend from the Purple Dragon, used any excuse to go out and celebrate.

Sid and Theo readily agreed. Aspen wanted to keep Sid here and talk about his impending death and the human ambassadors, but she didn't want to draw attention to the situation in front of Ella.

"Okay, let's take separate cars," Aspen said.

Ella rolled her eyes. "You get plenty of alone time with that one. Let's go together. I'll drive."

Sid grabbed Aspen's hand and pulled her close. "Sorry. I know you want to talk."

She glared at him. "You aren't sorry at all. You don't want to talk about it."

He grimaced. "You're probably right."

The air outside was frigid. Aspen was grateful that Ella's Bronco had warmed up on the way over. Aspen and Sid sat in the back seat, and he had his arm around her. She was a little ticked at him, but she could never resist his affection. When they got to the restaurant, a little steakhouse where Ella knew the owner so they got half-priced steaks, Aspen held Sid back.

"We need to talk," she said, resting on Ella's car. The cold metal made her shiver.

"I know," Sid said, leaning in to kiss her. She moved her head.

"I mean it."

"So you're withholding kisses until we talk about this?" He raised his eyebrows.

Aspen dropped her eyes. "No, but I want to know that you won't just avoid the subject."

Sid rested his forehead on hers. "I know you need answers, but this is not the place. Let's enjoy our time with our friends. Celebrate our victory. Then tomorrow I'll answer any of your questions. I promise. Now can I kiss you, please?"

She thought about saying no but couldn't think of good reason to. "Sure."

He kissed her hard, like he hadn't kissed her in ages. She forgot all about what she was irritated about and wondered why she would ever deny him a kiss.

CHAPTER 3

IT WAS THEIR first day back to school after the funeral. The hallways were eerily quiet. No longer could Sid hear laughter. Faces all had the same expression. Eyes were downcast, and no one smiled. Sid, himself, was sad. To lose two friends and a teacher in a matter of a few weeks was more than anyone should have to deal with, but Aspen had even more on her mind. Tori still wasn't speaking to her, and Sid knew Aspen was worried about him. She was knee deep in problems she couldn't even begin to fathom. Sid managed to avoid the topic over the last couple of days, since someone else was always around. But he knew eventually he'd have to come clean.

Aspen sat in front of him in homeroom. The substitute, Mr. Hudson, finally showed up. He had been a sub for math a few weeks prior, and he and Aspen had gotten off on the wrong foot. He checked the seating chart and narrowed his eyes.

"Aspen, that is not your seat."

"I know," she grumbled and moved up to the empty front row without a look back at Sid. Homeroom was only fifteen minutes. Sid hoped that the rest of the day wouldn't be like this. Mr. Hudson was going over announcements, and Sid let his thoughts wander. He was surprised when a voice entered his mind.

Hey, Obsidian. He'd know that voice anywhere.

Skye?

Surprise!

What? Sid's mind raced to comprehend what this meant. Where was she? Outside on top of the school? Why was she here?

I get to be human.

Sid only had a second to comprehend that information before she arrived in the doorway. Skye waltzed into the room every bit as gorgeous as a human as she had been as a dragon. Her platinum curls hung below her waist. She wore a lacy pink tank, and her denim skirt stopped in the middle of her tanned thighs. On some girls, it would look like she was trying too hard, but Skye appeared as if she just stepped out of a movie. She beamed when Mr. Hudson indicated to take the seat in front of Sid. Her long legs moved gracefully as she walked.

Sid had no idea what Skye was doing there. As only a half-royal, she was not supposed to have the human experience. She put her bag down next to her chair, and instead of sitting down, leaned over her desk and kissed him. Without thinking, he kissed her back and pulled her close. She smelled like the ocean. He'd missed her. Her kiss was so familiar, so comforting. So not Aspen. Sid broke away when Mr. Hudson spoke.

"Excuse me, Skye, I don't know where you came from. However, here in Gardiner we do not display our affections in school." There were titters and murmurs around the room.

"Sorry," she mumbled and slid down in her chair. Sid could not process what just happened fast enough. He flashed his eyes to the front of the room.

Aspen met his gaze for only a second before she turned her head away from him. He could see the tears on her cheeks. He opened himself up to feel her emotions. She was furious and hurt. He dropped his head so he didn't have to see her, shame burning his cheeks. He'd deal with her after homeroom. He couldn't do anything else here.

Skye, what are you doing here? Sid asked.

I came to keep you company, silly. Pearl told me all about your sealing issue and hoped that I could help you fix it.

CHAPTER 4

S CHOOL WAS A horrid, wretched place. Aspen didn't hear a word the teacher said in biology. She got to algebra early, in the hopes that she could get there before Sid and not have to see him. But she was out of luck. He was already in his seat. Aspen slid into her desk and didn't look back, but there was still two minutes until the bell rang. Maybe she should leave.

Sid tapped her on the shoulder, and she ignored him. She took a drink out of her water bottle, her hands shaking. Why the hell had he kissed that girl? He tapped again. She leaned forward. Finally, he got up and sat in the empty desk in front of her. She dropped her eyes so she didn't have to look at him.

"I'm sorry," he said.

Aspen glared at him. "You kissed her."

"She kissed me."

Aspen rolled her eyes. He was trying to get off on semantics.

"Yeah, I didn't see you in any hurry to break away."

Aspen tried to still her shaking hands. The water in the bottle sloshed a little. Her anger was getting the better of her. The seats around them were filling up. Class would start soon, and he wouldn't be able to talk to her anymore. If she could just last thirty seconds without losing it, she'd be fine.

"I know, it's just, I…"

"Don't you dare say you thought she was me."

His eyes flashed. "That's not what I was going to say." He got a weird smirk on his face. "I knew she wasn't you."

Yeah, that was worse. Aspen upturned her water bottle all over his head just as the bell rang. He sputtered. She stood up and gathered her books.

"Mrs. Weber, can I go to the nurse?"

Her teacher didn't even look up from the papers she was grading. "Sure."

Aspen managed to convince the nurse that she was really sick and needed to go home. She made it to her bedroom before totally losing it and lay down on her bed, pulled a pillow to her chest, and cried. How could Sid do this? She should've learned her lesson with Marc. This was almost worse because she should've been in control with this relationship. She withheld so much until she knew she could trust him, and then she'd given him everything. All of her heart and love.

Who was that girl? Was she a dragon too? Aspen had this nagging feeling she'd seen the girl before. She had to be a dragon. There was no way she could compete with beauty like that. Who knew the dragons would hurt her so bad?

"Hey, Aspen, you okay?"

Aspen's eyes flew open. Rowan stood over her. She sat up and pushed him back. "No, I'm not okay. What are you doing here anyway?"

"Tori told me what happened with Sid. Do you want to talk about it?"

"Not really. No offense or anything, but you're my brother. I don't particularly want to share my love life with you. I wish Sis were home."

He sat on the edge of her bed and stared at her. She knew he wasn't sure what to say.

"Yeah, me too. She always handled this stuff better than me. I still remember what happened down in Yosemite. I don't know what I would have done if she hadn't been home."

"You're making it worse." Rowan and Sissy had no idea what really happened in Yosemite. But they knew she'd had her heart broken. Her sister had been nursing her own broken heart by some surfer, so they spent the rest of that summer holed up in their cabin watching extremely violent movies to drown away their sorrows.

"Sorry. Come on, get dressed. I think I know how to make this better." Rowan tugged at her hand.

"How are you going to do that?"

"I'm not. Tori is on her way over. She said something about shopping therapy."

Aspen jumped up. "Tori's coming over?"

"Yeah, she'll probably be here in fifteen minutes."

Aspen stood on her wide front porch and tried to think of what she would say to Tori. It was really too cold to wait outside, but the chilly air cleared her mind. She needed to apologize to Tori but didn't know how.

Tori's Beetle pulled into the driveway, and Aspen climbed into the passenger seat. She was the one who'd screwed up.

"Tori, I'm really sorry about Sid. I didn't mean to hurt you."

"I know. You're forgiven. Friends are allowed to act foolishly where boys are concerned."

She knew she should be mad at Tori, but because she had no other close girlfriends at school, she wouldn't call Tori out for waiting until she was hurt to come back.

They drove into Bozeman and pulled up in front of Tori's favorite funky boutique. Tori knew all the good ones. Ella's friend owned it and took in donations like a thrift shop and then would modify them. She had serious talent. Of course her clothes were also crazy expensive, but Aspen wasn't looking to buy anything anyway.

Tori made a beeline for a rack of denim mini skirts that had patches of flannel sewn on them. Aspen's stomach clenched, thinking of that new girl at school. The one who stole Sid. Tori held one up to her and looked at Aspen, who grimaced.

"What?" Tori asked, looking down.

"Skye wore a miniskirt this morning."

Tori's face fell. "Oh, I'm sorry. Let's try something else."

"I'm not going to be good company today." Aspen thumbed through a rack of t-shirts, but she didn't really see them. This was probably a bad idea.

"Well then, we'll just have to figure out how to put you in a good mood." Tori just started grabbing various items off the rack and shoving them into Aspen's arms. "Come on, let's go try those things on."

"Why? It's not like I'm going to buy any of them."

Tori dug into her purse and waved a credit card in front of Aspen's face. "I have my mom's credit card and no restrictions. I've got to make up for ignoring you for the last couple of months. Let's find you something that will make Sid regret ever going back to that bitch. She hung all over him today. I even heard—"

Aspen held her hand up. "Stop. I don't want to hear anymore. Just give me the clothes."

Aspen pulled the curtain of the dressing room closed and took off her shirt, examining the choices in front her. She grabbed a blue t-shirt and got started on the pile of clothes.

Tori didn't try anything on, just kept pushing things at Aspen. They finally decided on a pair of skinny jeans that had been torn in various places and a Yale sweatshirt that fell off one of her shoulders.

Aspen was grateful for the distraction. Tori talked enough to make her forget everything else. It had been so long since they'd had girl time.

On their way home they stopped at the Purple Dragon.

Ella was putting chairs up on the tables. When Aspen asked for mochas, she groaned, but she started the espresso anyway.

"Where's your other half?" Ella asked.

Aspen tried to keep her voice from cracking as she spoke. "We broke up."

Ella dropped the milk container. "Crap. What happened?"

Aspen started to cry. What was wrong with her? She never cried before Sid came along, and now she was a freaking faucet.

Thankfully, Tori answered for her. "Some old bimbo girlfriend showed up. They made out in homeroom. Hudson had a tizzy. I heard she's even living at his house."

This was news to Aspen. "What else did you hear?" she asked.

"Oh, loads. She was in my math class, so I talked to her for a while. She's way sweet. I don't think she has any idea Sid has a girlfriend."

"Why didn't you mention this before?"

Tori leaned down to pet Wiggles. "I tried, but you said you didn't want to hear it."

Aspen crossed her arms as she processed this information. Suddenly, shopping for an outfit that would make Sid jealous seemed like a stupid idea. Skye was probably in some sexy piece of lingerie right now.

"I thought you were on my side."

"I am. I'm just telling you what I know. Anyway, they'd been together for a looong time. She said she'd missed him so bad that her parents arranged for her to come live here."

Ella mopped up the milk. "Are you sure things are over? Sid's totally smitten with you. Maybe she just took him by surprise."

Tori piped up. "He didn't leave Skye's side all day, unless they didn't have the same class. Trust me. Things are over."

"This seems out of character for him." Ella started the espresso.

Aspen clenched her fists. "Whatever. I can't work with him."

Ella handed over the mochas. "Don't worry, hun, I'll change the schedule. But I think you should talk to him."

Ella's words lingered in Aspen's mind. She had to admit this wasn't normal for Sid. Aspen didn't say much on the way home. When she got out of the car, she found Rowan on the porch. He waved to Tori, and she ignored him.

"You are pathetic. You know that, right? Tori's never gonna notice you." Aspen said and sat down next to him. "It's freezing out here. Why aren't you inside?"

"Mom and Dad are fighting."

Aspen grimaced. Rowan couldn't stand it when they fought. It didn't happen very often, though, and it usually dissipated quickly. Aspen thought they were probably safe to go back inside by now.

"So you figured you'd wait out here and get a glimpse of your illusive crush."

Rowan shook his head. "I don't really like her anymore."

"That's new."

"Yeah, so don't wig on me, but I've found someone more interesting." He dropped his eyes and picked at his fingernails.

"Why would I wig?"

"It's Skye."

"You mean the bitch who just stole my boyfriend? Why on earth would you do something like that? Not to mention the fact that she is *way* out of your league. Tori was top of the school pretty. Skye is hotter than most women in Hollywood. She knows how to flaunt it too. How on earth do you think you even stand a chance with her?"

"I told you not to freak out." Rowan's voice had gone very soft.

"Deal with it." Aspen clenched her fists. Why did everyone love this girl?

"Fine, I thought you might actually be pleased. For one thing, if I win her over, Sid will be left alone."

Aspen laughed. "I love you, bro, but you know that's never gonna happen."

"Well, she talks to me. Tori never did that. If you help me, I may actually have a shot."

"How could I possibly help? Wait, what do you mean, she talks to you?"

"I met her at Sid's party. She also sits by me in world civ, and we had a whole conversation. She's probably the nicest girl I've ever met."

That's where Aspen had seen her before. She'd bet her entire collection of dragon pics that Pearl was behind this. Aspen couldn't believe this was happening. A girl showed up today looking like a Victoria Secret model, stole the love of her life, and everyone thought she was a saint.

CHAPTER 5

S ID STORMED INTO the theater room when he got home, Skye on his heels. He couldn't help but talk to her during the day. She was comfortable, like coming home, and besides, this wasn't her fault. He found both Theo and Pearl sitting there.

Pearl grinned at Skye. "Was it as awesome as I told you it would be?"

Skye giggled and collapsed onto the couch next to Pearl.

Sid narrowed his eyes at both girls. "What are you talking about?"

Skye looked at him with her eyes dancing. "Kissing. We definitely have to do that again."

Fury burned in his chest. Pearl had set this all up.

"No, we don't. I have a girlfriend. Thanks to your kiss, she's not speaking to me. If you'll excuse me, I have to go figure out how to get her to forgive me." He pulled out his phone.

Pearl frowned and snatched his phone out of his hand. "No. You. Don't. Grow up, Sid. This isn't just some silly high school relationship.

You sealed yourself to her. You cannot take the chance that she'll seal herself to you. You're risking your entire kingdom. Hell, you're risking our entire existence." He reached for his phone, but she buried it in the couch.

"How's that?"

"I know you've been here having your human experience, but you being named king sent a small ripple through the dragon kingdom. You're well loved by most of the dragon races. But you managed to piss off the one dragon race who has never liked the royal dragons being in charge."

"The arctic dragons?"

"Yes. They are livid. The entire council flew up there to discuss your appointment. Most want you dead. I expect it is because they want a king they can control. Now, we know Prometheus and Raja would be good kings, and they support you, but Kingston has been spending a little too much time up north."

"If the council finds out about your sealing, they'll kill you, and Kingston could be the next king. There are no guarantees. Then what? You can't risk that. Not for any stupid girl."

Sid sank onto the couch, Aspen forgotten.

"I didn't know that Kingston had betrayed us."

"He hasn't yet, but it sure looks like he's doing the arctic dragons' bidding. If you die and he becomes king, we've essentially given them control over all of us." Pearl stood up. "I have to go. Do me a favor and make sure I don't have to show up here again. If I do this much more, the council is going to get suspicious. They had to approve Skye, so they are already on alert. Skye, keep an eye on him." Pearl pointed at Sid. "Obsidian, stay away from Aspen. I mean it."

She left the room, and Skye wouldn't meet his eye.

"Told you this would happen," Theo said.

"I'm not going to stay away from her."

"Did she see Skye kiss you?"

Sid nodded, picking up his phone again.

"Then your problem is fixed for you. Let it go. Skye can keep you company. I gotta run though. I'm spending the night at Ella's. See you two lovebirds later." He left the room, and Sid wished he could just erase the last forty-eight hours.

Skye sat a few feet from him. She hadn't said anything since he laid into Pearl. He closed his eyes. He wasn't angry with Skye, but he didn't love her anymore. Not the way she loved him, and he didn't want to give her the wrong idea. He also had to think of a way to get Aspen back.

"Can I show you something?" Skye asked, her voice soft.

He opened his eyes and looked at her. Her beauty took his breath away. It was different than Aspen's but anyone would appreciate her looks.

"Sure."

She took her boots off and then removed her socks. She put her feet in his lap, and he tensed.

"Look," she said.

He examined her ankles. "Your mark is gone."

She grinned. "Yep. That's why Pearl came to me. She thinks I can show you how to make yours go away too."

"What if I don't want it to go away?"

She shook her head at him. "You're in over your head."

"Maybe. She captured me in a way that I didn't think was possible."

Skye frowned. "I felt that way about you."

Sid leaned closer to her. "But you don't anymore?"

"Nope."

"I thought sealings took several years to fade."

She met his eyes. "You only think you know how they work, but I know more."

Sid smirked at her, enjoying the ease of their conversation. You don't spend a hundred and sixty-two years together and not be comfortable with one another. "Oh yeah, how's that?"

She frowned. "This isn't a happy story."

He leaned closer to her and brushed one of her platinum strands out of her face. "I'm sorry. I didn't want to cause you pain." He meant it. He still cared a great deal about her.

She took a deep breath. "I know. When Pearl asked me to come here, I said no. But you know how your sister is."

He laughed. "I do know. I want to hear your not-happy story though."

Her face was expressionless. He wished he could tell what she was thinking. He was surprised by how much he still cared for her. It was nothing compared to the way he felt about Aspen, but he didn't like to see her sad.

"When you became king, I was inconsolable. Beyond wrecked. Those first few days were pure agony. I wanted to die. But one day I woke up and realized I still had a choice. The unrequited sealing is so rare that most of us don't remember it's not permanent. I took my sadness and fury and channeled it into finding answers."

Skye was probably one of the best researchers he'd ever met. If answers were to be found, she'd find them.

"What'd you do?"

"I sought out every dragon who had ever had an unrequited sealing. Most of them had the same response. After several years of separation from the one they'd sealed themselves to, they would eventually stop pining for them, and the mark would fade."

That lined up with what Sid already knew. He was positive Skye had already known that as well.

"But that wasn't good enough for you, was it?"

She shook her head. "No. I thought of you constantly. It took every ounce of my willpower not to come here and ask you to go on the run with me. I missed you so much. I didn't want to wait several years for that to go away. I kept searching, and I found the one dragon who had all the answers. I can't tell you who he is. He made me promise if he would help me, that I wouldn't tell anyone about him. I intend to keep that promise."

Sid was curious, but he understood. "But will you tell me what he taught you?"

She nodded. "You already know there are three levels to the sealing. Most dragons skip step one and go straight to sealed, but the first one, the one where only one dragon loves the other, that's where anything can happen. It's not a true sealing.

"I was taught how each level worked, in detail. Beside the dragon who taught me, I probably know more about the sealings and the bondings than anyone else. Most sealings happen after years of love, and that is why they take so long to fade. But he taught me how to get rid of it instantly.

"I ran into Pearl a few days later and told her I'd gotten rid of it. That's why she sought me out when you got into your mess with Aspen. I don't know how she convinced the council to let me come, given our past, but then again, she's Pearl. She could convince a lizard he was a dragon."

Sid didn't care about any of that. He was still stuck on something she'd said minutes ago. There was only one dragon living that would have the answers she sought. "How'd you find Everett?"

"I never told you it was Everett."

"You didn't have to. Seriously, how'd you find him? He only comes out once every five hundred years, and there are dragons who are actively searching for him. No one can find him."

She bristled. "That is none of your business. Now show me your mark. I'd like to see it before you get rid of it."

"No."

"Why?" She pulled her legs out of his lap and tucked them underneath her.

"Well, for one thing, I'm not getting rid of it. For another, I'm not showing you."

Skye paled. "Sid, that could only mean—" She was interrupted by the doorbell ringing.

Sid looked at the clock on the wall. It was quarter to eleven. "Who's coming here this late?"

CHAPTER 6

ASPEN WASN'T SURE why in the world she was standing at Sid's door at eleven at night. Her parents had gone to bed after their fight, and she couldn't sleep. She had to figure all this out. She had to know where she stood with him. Where their relationship was going.

"We need to talk," she said when Sid answered the door. If he was surprised to see her, he didn't let on.

He nodded and moved aside for her to come in.

Aspen made a beeline for the theater room, and Sid followed. She stopped dead in the doorway. That girl. Skye. She was sitting on the couch with her bronzed legs curled underneath her.

Aspen turned back to Sid. "Is she like you?"

Sid nodded.

"What kind of dragon are you?" Aspen asked the girl.

Skye gasped. "She knows?"

"Aspen knows a lot of things. It's another reason why Pearl is so upset by all of this. Aspen, meet Skye, the dragon who rescued you from being eaten by alligators."

Aspen's eyes bugged and she covered her mouth. "You're that dragon? You're the reason I love dragons." Aspen felt her resolve shatter. She couldn't hate this girl even if she really wanted to. She knew she should sit down, but she stood in front of the couch, unable to move.

Skye grinned at her. "You've grown up. It's nice to meet you. I do want to apologize for kissing Sid earlier."

Aspen's anger came back. She crossed her arms and glared at Sid. "She had no idea you had a girlfriend. But you knew better. Why'd you kiss her back?"

He ran his hand through his hair and sighed. She'd hoped he'd have a good response, but he didn't say anything. She kicked off her shoes and ripped of her sock.

"Doesn't this mean anything to you? I thought you said it meant you'd never be able to love anyone ever again."

Skye squeaked from the couch, and Aspen looked over at her. Skye's face had gone white.

Sid pinched the bridge of his nose. "Skye didn't know about that."

He sat down next to Skye, and Aspen felt jealousy blossom in her chest. He took Skye's hand.

"No one knows, except maybe Theo. Please, you have to keep this secret for me."

Skye nodded. "Don't be mad at Aspen for showing me. I'd figured it out already when you wouldn't show me yours, but I hadn't really thought it was real. We'll deal with that problem later. Pearl is more likely to stay off your case if she thinks you are listening to me though. I'll help you hide your relationship, but it's going to have to be a secret."

Aspen raised an eyebrow. "Who said I want to stay in the relationship after today?"

Sid looked up, his face a mix of emotions. "You don't mean that."

"Maybe I do."

She backed up. She wasn't sure what she wanted anymore. She ran from the room, seeking fresh air, when a new voice entered her head.

He never looked at me the way he looks at you.

Aspen hesitated just long enough for Sid to catch up with her. He grabbed her hand and pulled her close to him. She thought about running again, but Skye distracted her.

I know you can't feel his guilt, but I can. The second after I kissed him, he felt awful, and he hasn't stopped feeling that way since. He's got a long road ahead of him. The dragons are facing things they haven't had to deal with in over a thousand years. He needs you by his side. If you leave him now, he's as good as dead, and the dragons need him as their leader, even if no one else sees that.

Aspen tried to make sense of her words but couldn't. Especially not with Sid holding her against him. She became aware of his breathing and the warmth of his body. He traced his finger across her face, and she shivered. He lifted her chin so that she was looking right up at him.

"Aspen Winters, I love you, and I'll do whatever it takes to keep you in my life."

She didn't even think. It was like they were on the side of the road again that day when Aspen first kissed him. She stood up on her tiptoes and crushed her lips against his. He responded immediately this time, wrapped his arms around her waist, and lifted her up. She lost all sense of space and time in that kiss. In that moment she knew she could never give him up.

CHAPTER 7

THE NEXT DAY at school, Skye met Aspen outside their homeroom. They agreed that the best way to keep the dragons out of their business was for Skye and Sid to pretend to be together. But in order to keep Aspen close, she would befriend Skye. Aspen knew Tori wouldn't buy it, but she had plans for that too.

Skye and Aspen chatted for a few minutes before Tori walked up to them.

She looked at them dubiously. "Hey," Tori finally said.

"You were right, she is super sweet," Aspen said.

Tori raised her eyebrows. "Sure."

Sid walked by them, and Skye chased after him. Aspen tried to ignore the feelings of jealousy that crept up every time she looked at them together. They had to do this.

Tori frowned. "What was that all about?"

"I went over to Sid's last night to figure out what was going on, and Skye and I talked for a long time. As much as I want to, I can't hate her."

"Bull. What's really going on?"

Aspen dropped her voice down to a whisper. "Skye's never gonna give him up. But if I befriend her, then I stay close to Sid. I just need to show that I'm better for him than Skye. I can be patient."

Tori nodded. "That sounds like the Aspen I know. Can I help? Gather dirt and all that?"

"Sure. I can use all the help I can get."

In algebra, Sid leaned forward and brushed Aspen's hair off her bare shoulder and whispered into her ear.

"How am I supposed to keep my hands off you when you look so damn sexy?"

He traced a finger along her neck and then leaned back in his chair. Aspen shivered. She turned and grinned.

"Tori and I went shopping, and she wanted to make sure you knew what you were missing out on."

He winked at her. "Well, it worked."

After school, Aspen followed Sid and Skye to the Purple Dragon. She wanted to tell Ella to forget changing the schedule. Plus, Ella was pretty good at spotting bullshit, so if they could convince her that they were just friends, they could convince anyone.

Sid held Skye's hand as they entered the coffee shop, and Aspen had to fight off her jealousy. She knew there was nothing between them, but try telling that to her emotions. Ella was cleaning out the espresso machine, which meant she was covered in coffee.

"Hey, Ella," Aspen said.

"Hey." She looked up and blinked when she saw Sid and Skye. "Who's this?" she asked, nodding to Skye.

"This is my girlfriend, Skye," Sid said.

Ella crossed her arms and glowered at the two of them. "Last I checked Aspen was your girlfriend."

"No, it's okay. Really, it's why we came. You don't have to change the schedules. Sid and I can work together. In fact we'd like to."

Ella raised an eyebrow at Aspen. "Something stinks."

"Skye is really sweet," Aspen continued, hoping she'd convince Ella.

Ella glared at Skye. "That seems to be the word that everyone uses to describe you."

Skye shrugged. "Maybe it's true. It is nice to finally meet you. Everyone's said good things about you. You're Theo's girl, aren't you? He seems pretty smitten."

"Just because everyone else likes you doesn't mean I have to." Ella went back to wiping the counter like they weren't there.

Sid moved closer to Skye and pulled her into his side. "I think we'll be going. Aspen are you coming over later to tackle that algebra?"

"Yeah, give me an hour or so."

He nodded to her and walked back toward the door with his arm around Skye. Aspen watched them until they disappeared out the door, trying to stave off the jealousy she felt when they were together.

"You're not okay with this. I can tell."

Aspen turned to face Ella. She hated that Ella could see right through her. "No really, I understand. They'd been together a long time. Sid and I were better as friends anyway."

Ella shook her head. "No, you weren't. But I won't change the schedules in the hopes that you'll steal him back from that blonde bitch."

Rowan stopped Aspen just as she was heading out the door.

"Where are you going?"

"To Sid's."

He creased his eyebrows. "I thought you broke up."

"We did, but decided to stay friends. He's helping me with my math homework."

Rowan fidgeted with his zipper. "Can I come with? Maybe tackle some of my world civ homework with Skye."

Aspen leaned down to tie up her boots. "Rowan, seriously. You need to give it up."

"Whatever."

He headed for the living room, and Aspen immediately felt bad. He'd never really had a whole lot of friends because of his social anxiety.

"You can come with."

He turned, and his eyes lit up. "Really?"

"Yeah, come on."

He was twitchy in the car, tapping his finger on the window and bouncing his knee.

"You gonna be okay?" Aspen finally asked.

"Of course."

They arrived at the mansion a few minutes later.

"I still can't get over the size of this house," said Rowan.

"I know. It looks a lot different than it did at Halloween."

They went through the kitchen to the breakfast room. It was cozy with a large round table and lots of natural light. Skye had books spread out in front of her. Sid was lying on the window seat.

Skye looked up when they walked in. "Hey, you brought Rowan." She beamed at him, and Aspen rolled her eyes. She'd have to warn Skye not to break his heart. Aspen sat by Sid, and he snaked his arm around her waist. She moved it.

"You ready to tackle that algebra homework?"

Sid sat up and looked over at Rowan and Skye, who were already in a discussion about World War II.

"Yeah, let's take it upstairs so we aren't interrupted."

Aspen's stomach flip-flopped. Sid grabbed his book, and Aspen followed him up the stairs. He pulled her into the room, and as soon as the door was shut, he planted his lips on hers, and she melted into him.

After what seemed like forever, she pulled away. He leaned his forehead on hers.

"I hate that we can't do that in public anymore."

"I know. Sorry about Rowan."

Sid shrugged. "Bring him anytime. He's a nice kid. Skye likes him too."

Aspen sat on the bed and fingered her math book. "We probably should get some of this homework done."

Sid crawled across the bed to her. "Yeah. I can do that later, after you leave. I can't do this then." He pressed his lips against her neck, and she shivered.

"No, I don't expect you can do that after I'm gone." Aspen giggled and shoved the book on the floor.

An hour or so later, they finally went back downstairs and found Rowan and Skye in the theater room.

"What happened to homework?" Sid asked, sitting next to Skye.

"We finished. You guys get that algebra done?" Skye wiggled her eyebrows, and Rowan gave her a strange look.

"Sure did," Sid said with a grin, and Aspen blushed.

"You guys want to stay for dinner? We could order pizza," Skye said.

"Sure," Aspen replied. "If that's okay with you." Aspen turned to Rowan, and he nodded, never taking his eyes off Skye. Aspen sighed and texted her parents that they wouldn't be home for dinner.

Theo walked in, dressed in a t-shirt and gym shorts with his dreads pulled back. He thumped Sid on the shoulder.

"The gym calls. You coming?"

"Nope. I've got company."

"Come on, bro, it's only thirty minutes. Aspen's here all the time." He bounced on the balls of his feet.

Skye spoke up. "We can order pizza while you guys work out. Go ahead."

Sid stood. "If I have to go, so does Rowan."

Rowan shook his head and finally looked away from Skye. "Not my thing. Thanks."

Skye laughed. "A little muscle never hurt anyone."

Rowan didn't hesitate. He jumped off the couch and followed Sid and Theo out of the room.

Aspen waited until the boys were out of earshot. "You know he's madly in love with you, right?"

Skye raised her eyebrows. "Rowan? No way. We're friends."

"Maybe for you, but you are the first female in three years to voluntarily speak to him, and you're gorgeous. He's head over heels."

Skye undid her braid and ran her fingers through her hair. "He's beautiful. Why don't girls talk to him?"

"Because of his nerves. If you don't make eye contact with someone, they aren't likely to talk to you."

"He always looks at me."

Aspen thought for a minute. It was true. She'd never known Rowan to speak with anyone who wasn't part of the family. Occasionally he spoke to Tori, but she was around so often that it would be awkward if he didn't.

"I know. It's weird. But just be careful. I don't want him getting hurt."

Skye nodded. "Okay. I'm not looking to fall in love with anyone. Especially not after what happened with Sid."

"About that. Exactly what did happen?" Aspen was starting to get used to Skye being here and wasn't quite as jealous, but she was curious about their past.

"He became the king, and I could never be queen."

"Why not?"

"This is something you should ask Sid about, not me." Skye studied her fingernails and picked the polish on her thumb.

"I have. He won't tell me." Now Aspen was really curious. Sid didn't like to talk about the whole queen thing.

Skye wouldn't meet Aspen's eyes. "Then I probably shouldn't either. But I can tell you this, the queen has to have certain qualities that I don't have."

"What kind of qualities?" Aspen was suddenly optimistic about getting answers.

"She has to have reached maturity, come from a family with strong leadership, and have several brothers and sisters."

"Why lots of brothers and sisters?"

"Posterity."

Aspen had heard that word before, but she had no idea what it meant. "I don't understand."

"They want him to be able to have lots of kids so the royal line can live on."

"But Sid told me about how he became king, and he wasn't the king's son."

"It's still a requirement. Don't ask me to try to understand the inner workings of the dragon council. Most of what they do doesn't make sense."

Skye shifted in her seat. Sound burst out of the speakers, and an explosion appeared on the wall. Skye jumped up, and Aspen grabbed the remote she'd sat on.

They both laughed, and nothing more was said about kings and queens, though Aspen couldn't help but feel that she was missing something extremely important.

Thirty minutes later, the doorbell rang and Skye ran to get it. While Aspen waited for Skye to get the pizza, the boys came back into the room, all sweaty.

Aspen looked up. "Enjoy your workout?"

Sid nodded and wiped a towel across his forehead. "I'm gonna go change."

Rowan looked green. As soon as Sid and Theo disappeared upstairs, he collapsed on the floor and lay there, not moving.

"You okay?" Aspen asked.

Rowan shook his head. "They are animals. I couldn't keep up with them if I tried."

"We can cross personal trainer off your list of possible careers then, huh?"

"Theo should consider it. He yelled at me the whole time I was in the gym."

Aspen stood over Rowan. "You gonna come eat?"

Rowan nodded and held out his hand. Aspen pulled him up, and he groaned. His face was flushed, and his hair was all sweaty. "You might want to go wash up. There's a bathroom just outside the kitchen."

Aspen helped Skye gather plates and cups. A few minutes later all three boys appeared. Theo patted Rowan on the back.

"You're coming tomorrow, right?"

Rowan swallowed and looked at Skye, who smiled at him.

"We should do this every day. Homework, workout, and dinner," Skye said.

"I'll be here." Rowan gave Skye a grin.

Aspen nearly choked on her pizza. He was so in for it.

In the car, on the way home, she tried to feel him out.

"You don't have to come tomorrow."

"I know. I want to."

"She's not looking for a relationship. She's with Sid." Skye didn't seem like the type to intentionally hurt someone, but she'd rip his heart out without even realizing what she'd done.

Rowan snorted. "Yeah right. Sid still has eyes only for you. I'm not sure what's going on. But he and Skye are not together. Show me your algebra homework because I expect it's not done."

"I left my book at Sid's." Aspen thought for a few seconds on how to handle this. Admit that something was going on or deny it? If Rowan would be spending more time at Sid's, then keeping it a secret would be difficult. "Please don't tell anyone. It's important people think Skye and Sid are together."

"I don't suppose you'll tell me what's really going on."

"Not yet."

He frowned at her. "You can trust me."

"I do. But it's not my secret to share."

"Whatever. But I'm not just going over there for Skye. I was beat after the workout, but my anxiety was all but gone. It was amazing."

"Huh. Maybe you should've started that earlier."

CHAPTER 8

A COUPLE OF WEEKS later, Rowan collapsed on the couch again after their workout. Sid sat down next to him, his own t-shirt soaked in sweat.

"You okay?" Sid asked.

Rowan nodded and wiped at his forehead. He flexed his arm, showing a hint of muscle. "That's never been there before." He gave Sid a grin.

Sid laughed. "I'm sure Skye will be impressed."

Rowan scowled. "I'm not ready to show her yet. But we're getting there."

"She likes you."

"That's not what Aspen says."

"Aspen just doesn't want you to get hurt. Though, I'll admit, Skye's feelings are probably pretty platonic. She's not ready to jump into anything."

Rowan lay down and closed his eyes. "I can be patient."

"I'm gonna go shower."

"I think I'm going to stay here for a few minutes before I shower. Theo was an animal today. My legs are still shaking."

Sid was surprised by how much Rowan changed in the last couple of weeks. He seemed almost relaxed when he was around them now.

Sid showered and found Aspen and Skye in the kitchen.

"Whatcha making?" he asked Skye.

"Cheesecake." She pointed to the iPad on the counter where some YouTube chef demonstrated how to whip the cream cheese. Sid let out a breath of relief. At least it wasn't dinner. Two days after Skye arrived, she discovered YouTube cooking videos and was hooked. She spent almost all her free time in the kitchen. She nailed desserts but everything else was disastrous. Course Rowan would scarf down anything she made, but the rest of them ran from the kitchen if she was making anything other than something sweet.

Theo walked into the kitchen with a bag slung over his shoulder.

"Oh, man, cheesecake. Save me a piece."

"Where are you going?" Skye asked.

"Ella's."

Skye scowled. She didn't like Ella, but that was probably because Ella still gave her the cold shoulder. Aspen tried to explain that everything was fine, but things were still icy between them, which was why Theo was spending the night at Ella's instead of the other way around.

Aspen watched Skye stirring the ingredients and then looked up at Sid. He smiled at her.

"Why do you have to die?" Aspen asked out of nowhere.

Sid sat down next to her. "Where'd this come from? I thought we talked about this."

"You promised to explain, but you didn't. Then Skye showed up, and we haven't really had time to talk. I tried to get her to tell me, but she wouldn't either. This is the first time we've been alone enough to discuss it because Rowan is always around."

Sid looked at Skye, who seemed to be deliberately staring at her bowl. So much for help from her.

"Did you know thirty years ago Skye sealed herself to me?"

Aspen jerked her head around. "What?" She went around the counter. "Show me your ankle."

Skye smiled. "I could, but there's nothing there anymore."

"I thought the marking was forever."

"It is, if both dragons love each other. But if it is only one, then the marking can fade away," Skye said.

"How long does it take?"

"Ten to fifteen years," said Sid. "Skye did something to make hers go away instantly, but she won't tell me how."

She dipped her finger in the cheesecake mix and tasted it.

"What happened is none of your business. If I thought it could help you, I'd tell you, but it won't, so it doesn't matter. Maybe you should actually try telling Aspen the whole truth instead of just part of it."

"What's she talking about?" Aspen asked, her eyes flashing.

"Yeah, Sid, explain to her exactly why you never sealed yourself to me."

Sid glared at Skye. She was making this so much harder than it had to be. He wasn't ready for Aspen to know everything about what being the dragon king meant. If she knew everything, she might do something stupid. He'd have to leave out certain details. Like the one way she could make it work so that no one had to die. Except maybe her.

"This is an extremely long story. Are you sure you want to hear it?"

Aspen laughed. "I'm not going anywhere. The best thing about Rowan going out with me is that I no longer have to worry about being out late. I'll just send a text and tell my parents that we're pulling an all-nighter here. They're so tickled Rowan's out with friends that they won't care."

Sid blinked for a second at the implications. They'd only spent one night together, and that was in the freezing cold mountains. He swallowed and tried not to think about what was coming after he finished his story. He scooted his chair closer to her and thought for a minute of where to start this story.

"The year I was born, there were only five royal sons born. We all have different parents, but from the beginning, we were special."

"Why?" Aspen leaned forward in her chair, and Sid tried not to think about how her lips felt on his. He scooted away in order to keep his thoughts straight, because he had to be very careful not to give too much away.

"Because that was the year the king chose his death. It would be five hundred years from then. All kings do it. It is so that whoever the future king is will be prepared. There was myself, Theo, Marcellus, Raja, and Kingston. From our infancy we were trained for the possibility."

"Wait. Your parents named you Obsidian. Why would they do that if you were gold?"

"Because I was born after the king declared his death. All of us were. The king made the announcement at the beginning of the year. My parents had high hopes."

Aspen rocked back in her chair. "I want to meet your parents."

Skye coughed. "Probably not a good idea."

Aspen swiveled around to face her. "Why not?"

"Sid's parents hated me because they felt I threatened his kingship. If they thought for a second that Sid was going to die because of you, they'd kill you themselves. Trust me, you do not want to meet his parents. His dad is okay, but his mom has a temper."

"I'm confused." Her eyebrows creased. Sid wanted to kiss that spot on her forehead where they came together. But he had to get this story out, or she'd bug him until he did.

"Can I finish?"

"Oh, yeah, continue." Aspen settled back in her chair and set her hand on his knee. He swallowed and refocused his thoughts.

"Anyway, we trained and went on with our lives. The other four made sure they got their human experience over with. I was with Skye and didn't want to leave her, but everyone knew the king was about to die. It's not an exact timing. There is usually a fifteen to twenty year range in which he could die. Skye and I just decided that I should get the human experience over with when the king died. We expected him to live another several years. But he died early.

"Theo should've been king. Not me. Hell, even Raja would've made a better king than me. But I was the one chosen."

"By who?"

"No one knows. All we know is that when the king dies, one of the potential heirs becomes king. We figured the gods would pick whomever was the best suited for the job. But I was the lucky one who turned black. Prometheus was furious."

"Who's Prometheus?"

Sid laughed. "Theo." He leaned back in the chair, still frustrated by the turn of events. He wished he knew what the hell he'd done to get picked.

Aspen twirled a piece of her hair and pursed her lips. "No wonder he's goes by Theo. What an awful name. If you didn't plan on becoming king, why didn't you just seal yourself to Skye?"

"Because I knew becoming king was a possibility. I didn't want to die or risk the dragon wars again."

"I've never heard of the dragon wars."

"They were thousands of years of ago."

"Why would you sealing yourself to the wrong dragon cause them?"

"Because a king is only as strong as his queen, and Skye could never be my queen. If I flouted tradition and sealed myself to her, then I'd open myself up as a weak king since I had no queen. It'd be a mess, really. Well, it will be a mess anyway. I don't reign, not yet. I cannot take my place as the rightful king until my queen is presented to me. Pearl is out searching for her. It will be a few years before one is found and ready. The problem is, that name on my ankle was meant for my queen, not you. And so when I am discovered, I will be killed for ruining the kingship, and another king will be found."

"At least Skye is a dragon."

"Being a dragon has nothing to do with it. To keep the peace, all the dragon races have a say in who the queen is to keep the peace. Then there is the testing."

Sid shivered, and Skye squeaked.

Aspen's eyes widened. "What's wrong with the testing?"

"Most potential queens die. The king before me had to watch four possibilities before one finally survived."

"That sounds awful."

"I've heard it is. I've never witnessed it. I guess I won't either since I can't have a queen."

Skye spoke up. "Then why is Pearl out searching for one?"

"Because she doesn't know you've sealed yourself to me."

Aspen frowned. "If you're supposed to be king, why don't you just take the throne anyway? I mean, it seems stupid to let them kill you. Stand up for yourself. Isn't that what kings do?"

"That would cause a war."

Aspen didn't understand. She couldn't, and Sid didn't know how to express how dire this was. Sid's stomach became a tight knot. Even the mere thought of thousands of dragons dying caused him to want to flee.

"Isn't it worth it?"

Sid frowned. How could she be so callous about this? She was talking about a war. One that if it started, would be his fault.

"You don't know what you are talking about."

Aspen stood and got right in his face. "You were chosen to be king for a reason. Show them what you are made of. Fight for yourself."

"It's not that easy."

Her face flushed, and Sid felt a tightening in his chest that came from her.

She crossed her arms and backed away, her eyebrows arched. "Oh, yeah, then I guess you deserve to die. No real king would do that."

She stormed out of the room. A few seconds later he heard the front door slam.

"She didn't mean it," Skye said softly.

"I know. I felt her fear as well as you did. She's scared for me." Sid sank down onto one of the kitchen chairs. He didn't know how to get out of this. Aspen was right. He was going to die. He was a coward.

"As she should be. I'm scared for you too."

Skye sat across from him.

"She doesn't know what she's talking about," Sid said.

"Maybe not, but she's right." Skye wrapped her hands around his and gave him a small smile.

"What do you mean?" She wasn't making sense. How could she think that Aspen was right? She was talking about starting a war.

"Traditions change all the time. Why can't you rule without a queen? You and Aspen can stay together until she dies, and you can still be a good king." Skye squeezed his hands and stared at him with her wide blue eyes.

"I'll be weak, though, because I'll have no queen."

"So make her your queen."

Sid laughed. "Yeah, right. I can't do that, and you know it. Every possibility I've thought of ends with both of us dying."

"Nope. There's another way."

"What are you talking about?"

"It's old magic, dating back to the dragon wars. Surely you know what I mean."

"The loyalty circle?"

"Yep."

"Skye, those seals caused thousands of dragons to die last time. I'll not invoke it again."

"We're looking at a war anyway. You might as well give yourself a fighting chance. Look, it won't be that hard to gain your supporters. You've got me, Theo can represent the royal tribe, you know Damien will give you allegiance from the fire dragons, and Darneil will help you without question. That's four out of the eight without a fight. Jolantha will probably help as well. That's five. That leaves canyon, river, and arctic."

"But it won't work unless I get them all."

"I know, but if you do, the council will have no choice. They'll have to step down and acknowledge the council of your own choosing."

"Do you know how many dragons tried this during the dragon wars?"

"Yeah, but leadership was up for grabs at that point. Right now, no one knows anything. You should be able to do it quietly, and no one has to die. Including you. War would be avoided."

"If this doesn't work, whoever gives me their loyalty will die."

She shrugged. "I'd do it for you."

"You love me."

"So do a lot of others. You can't see why you were made king, but I can. You are personable, and you care deeply for others. Even now, you are thinking about what is best for the dragons, not yourself."

"I don't think this will work. I'm not going to ask other dragons to die for me."

"They only die if you don't succeed."

"The probability of my success is low. Why should I risk that?"

"For Aspen? She'll die along with you. You know this. If you won't do this for yourself, do this for her. Besides, I think you are underestimating yourself."

"You'd really be willing to give up your life for me?"

Skye leaned forward and whispered in his ear. "I don't expect you to fail." She kissed him on the cheek and held out her hand for him. "Come on, let's get this started."

Sid wasn't even sure he knew how to invoke the ancient magic. Once he began, he couldn't quit. This was one sealing that couldn't fade or be removed. He had to have all the races too or it wouldn't work. After he secured his first seal, he only had until someone spotted the marks on one of the other dragons. Skye was safe. So were Damien and Theo. But the rest. He'd also have to ask them to go into hiding. That wasn't fair to ask of them, but he supposed if they were willing to die for him, they'd be willing to hide for him.

If the council found out, they'd be livid, and they'd kill him straight-away. If he succeeded in securing all eight races, he'd have a full circle, and the council would be forced to step down.

They went out into the backyard and both transformed into their dragon forms.

I'm not sure how this works, Sid said.

Lucky for you, I do. Remember, I spent the last few months hanging out with Everett. He taught me a lot. You don't have to do anything. When we are finished, I'll explain how it works, though, so you can help the others. Are you ready?

Skye, are you sure? If this doesn't work, you will die. You know that.

I know. Lower your head please. I can't reach it.

He did as she asked.

Obsidian, on behalf of the sea dragons, I pledge our loyalty to you and only you.

She touched her snout to his forehead, and he felt a thread of warmth flow from his head to a spot on his chest that burned.

She backed up. He swung his head around and tried to look down at his chest but couldn't see anything. He looked back at Skye.

This means the world to me.

Obsidian, the world would be a sad place if you weren't in it. I believe in you. Others will too. On her own chest a circle had appeared with his name in the center. She'd just given up one sealing and gained another one. Though this one was far more dangerous.

They turned back into their human forms, and Sid held her hand as they walked back inside. He did love her, not romantically, but she was one of his best friends, and now she'd pledged her life to him. The depth of her devotion was beyond comprehension. It would be worth it if he could complete the new council. Otherwise, they'd all die.

Skye was right though, and if he could get one dragon from each dragon race to pledge loyalty to him, then he'd be able to take over. Only one dragon in history had ever succeeded, and it was the king who ended the dragon wars. Maybe Sid would be able to stop these wars before they even begin.

Back in the house, he took off his shirt and stared at the blue circle that appeared on his chest. In the middle of the circle was Skye's name, and he tried to make sense of the writing around it, but it was their ancient tongue and hard to read in the mirror. Skye would have to help him translate it in the morning.

CHAPTER 9

ASPEN WAS STILL angry when she woke up the next morning. What right did Sid have to think he could just die? There had to be another way. Her phone buzzed a few minutes later.

Want to go for a ride?

I'm still mad.

I know. But I want to show you something. Meet me in the grove we used to meet in.

Stay mad at Sid or go for a dragon ride? That was tough. Aspen ignored the phone and hopped in the shower instead. She'd go for a ride with him, but she was going to let him sweat it out first.

When she got out of the shower, there were thirty texts from him all basically saying the same thing.

I'm sorry.

She sighed and texted him back.

I know. Meet me in thirty.

She was lacing up her boots when Rowan met her in the doorway.

"Where are you going?" He brushed his hair out of his eyes. Aspen saw his muscles in his arms flex. Hanging with Sid and Theo had been good for him.

Aspen almost said, "to see Sid." But then she remembered that Rowan wasn't privy to all their secrets yet. He didn't know Sid was a dragon.

"I haven't seen my dragon in a while. I'm going for a ride." She stood up and grabbed the door handle.

"Can I come? You said I could meet him." Damn. She'd forgotten about that.

"Maybe another time. It's been ages since I've been able to hang with him."

"Please, I won't stay long. I just want to meet him." He took his glasses off and rubbed his eyes. He looked younger without them.

"Why? You're doing so much better. Why risk it? It is a dragon after all."

"That's the point, though, isn't it? If I can meet a dragon without freaking out, maybe I'll get over this."

Aspen wasn't sold on the idea. She hoped Sid would say no. If Sid didn't allow Rowan to come meet him as a dragon, then Aspen didn't have to be afraid of what the meeting might do to him. Rowan was scared of a lot of things, but the thing he feared most were dragons. He couldn't even stand looking at Aspen's pictures. Meeting Obsidian could put him in a comatose state.

"Alright, come on. But you should probably wait out of sight until I make sure it's okay." Sid as a dragon always behaved a little differently than Sid the man. She had no idea what he would say.

Aspen got to the clearing first. She watched Sid fly low and fast. He landed hard. His claws left two craters in the ground. His huge body was heaving as if he had been running.

"What's the rush?" Aspen asked.

I didn't want to be late.

"Late? You got here less than ten minutes after me, and I was early."
She smiled at him. She still couldn't believe he was hers.

I don't want to make you wait.

Aspen stared up at his chest. A brilliant blue circle that had not been there before was bright against his black scales. Right in the middle was the word "Skye."

"Why do you have Skye's name on your chest?" Aspen's heart clenched. The only other name he had on his body was hers. What did it mean?

Long story, but it has to do with keeping me alive. Let's go for a flight, and I'll explain everything. I've invoked some ancient magic.

Aspen wanted more than anything to climb on his back and learn what all of this was about, but Rowan was hiding out in the trees.

"We can't." She waved his head down. "First, we need to talk."

Sid felt a great deal of anxiety coming from Aspen. He spoke before she could get a word out.

Have I told you about the gifts of the dragons?

"No." She took a couple of steps back and cocked her head.

Each dragon race is given a special gift. The river dragons can speak out loud, and the arctic dragons live longer than the rest of us. We, the royal dragons, are given the gift of feeling.

"What does that mean?" She cocked her head.

It means that I can feel what you are feeling. It's not mind reading. It's feeling.

"So when I'm really happy, you can feel my happiness."

Exactly.

She raised her eyebrows. "Wow. So what was I feeling the first time I saw you?"

Excitement, awe, and elation.

She nodded. "Sounds about right. Does that mean anytime I want to make out with you, you can tell?"

Sid shifted a little. *Yeah.*

She laughed. "What about now?"

Fear, you are scared. I don't understand why. And he didn't. He rarely felt fear from her. Maybe she was still worried about his death.

"Oh, well, I have to ask you something, and I am afraid of your response."

Are you afraid I will eat you or something? He snorted, and black smoke escaped from his nostrils.

"It's about Rowan. He saw us together a while ago. I forgot about it until he reminded me as I was leaving."

Has he told anyone? Rowan was getting more and more involved in their lives. If Sid wasn't careful, Rowan's life would be on the line as well.

"Oh no, he wouldn't do that. He only told me. The thing is, he wants to meet you."

Sid was amused. Rowan, the boy who, until two weeks ago, could hardly walk out his front door, wanted to meet him as a dragon?

Why?

"Honestly, I don't know. Would it be alright? Will you meet with him?"

When?

"Right now, if you're willing."

Why not?

Aspen patted Sid's flank and hurried off down the path. A few minutes later she came back alone.

Well, where is he? Sid asked her.

"Hidden in that stand of pines. He won't come any closer right now. Maybe you can talk him into coming out."

Sid supposed he could do that, but Rowan would expect that. Sid recalled when Rowan was with Theo, and the harder Theo rode him, the harder he worked out. Sid decided to do something unexpected, something blunt.

He aimed a volley of flames directly over the stand of pines, singeing the top of the trees. Rowan did not appear.

Aspen flung herself at him, arms flailing. "You idiot! What was that for? He's probably wet himself now. What on earth were you thinking? I told you he was scared. If you didn't want to see him, you could have just said so."

Distracted by Aspen's tirade, Sid didn't see Rowan come out, but Sid felt him as he approached. Never before had he experienced the sheer terror he felt now. Sid's body shook, and breathing became a challenge. Sid took deep heaving breaths.

Aspen, stop.

She continued pounding on his underbelly. "You jerk. I can't believe you did that to him!"

Aspen, he is coming closer. I cannot have you beating on me like a punching bag. STOP.

She stopped. Sid's shaking and rapid breath did not. He couldn't quite believe that Rowan could be walking so calmly while feeling so horrid. Sid knew if he got closer, it would only make matters worse.

Rowan, please do not come any closer.

"Why?"

I feel what you are feeling.

Rowan sat on the ground about thirty feet from Sid. "What do my feelings have to do with getting any closer?"

You're terrified.

"Yeah, so, I'm always afraid. It is my perpetual state of being. This whole mind speak thing is pretty cool."

How do you even function? I'm not you, yet I shake with fear.

"I'm used to it. It never really goes away. It's amplified now because I'm faced with a real freaking dragon, but this really isn't all that much worse than usual."

Rowan Winters, you are no coward.

He laughed. "You feel my terror. How could you possibly say that?"

Can you see me?

"Yes."

Sid was still baffled that Rowan could carry on the conversation like nothing was wrong. *Can you not see that I am shaking?*

"Yes."

I am shaking because of your fear. I am feeling what you feel, and I cannot tolerate it. Yet here you sit speaking to me as if nothing is wrong. You face me in spite of your fears. You are braver than most men and a few dragons as well.

Rowan smiled, and Sid's body stopped trembling. Rowan got up and slowly made his way toward him. Sid remembered Skye's mark and dropped to the ground. Rowan froze when Sid moved, but Sid didn't want to answer any questions about the mark.

Come on, I'm not going to hurt you.

Rowan took a couple of deep breaths and moved so he was standing next to Sid, then he placed a hand on Sid's neck. Aspen had tears flowing down her cheeks.

Didn't you tell me you never cry?

"Shut up."

Rowan hung out with Sid and Aspen for the morning. He turned down Sid's offer of a ride, and Sid figured it was for the best. No sense pushing his luck.

"Why do you have my sister's name on your ankle?" Rowan sat next to Sid's foot and traced the letters above his heel. Aspen settled next to him, her head resting on Sid's flank with her eyes closed. Her face was peaceful and serene.

It's complicated. But she has my name on hers, and in a sense it means we are forever bound to each other.

"That's cool. So you are her protector or something?"

I guess you could say that.

"Does that mean the other dragons know about her?"

Aspen's eyes popped open. "Do you ever see any other dragons when you are out flying? You shouldn't be here. Maybe we should stop these visits."

Relax, no one has seen it yet.

"That's right. You'll just wimp out and die when they discover it."

Rowan looked at her with his eyebrows creased. Aspen crossed her arms and pouted. Sid would find it cute if she wasn't so terrified by the prospect. He never thought about what his death would do to her. He hadn't planned on Rowan showing up today, so he put off his visit to Damien, but tomorrow they'd start trying to save both of their lives.

We need to meet tomorrow. I have something to show you. Meet here, same time?

"Sure." She shrugged and looked away from him. "We should go. See you tomorrow."

CHAPTER 10

ASPEN WANTED TO go over to Sid's house that afternoon, but her parents said they never spent any time at home anymore and had to spend the day with them. After a Skype call to Sissy in Hawaii, they went into Bozeman, did some shopping, had dinner, and caught a movie.

The next day Sid was about thirty minutes late. He was breathless, but not agitated.

Sorry, I'm late. Skye tried making sweet potatoes in the oven, and it caught on fire. I just spent the last hour airing out the kitchen. Theo's going to buy a new oven.

Aspen laughed. "Sweet potatoes? In the morning?"

They had marshmallows on them, and she loves marshmallows.

Aspen shook her head. One of these days Skye would burn down his whole house.

Hop on. We are going for a ride.

"Where?"

You'll see.

Aspen climbed on his back, and he took off. She clung to his neck and watched the ground disappear beneath her. Yellowstone looked completely different from up there. The colors on the ground all swirled together. The hot springs burned a bright blue and the white ground around them was speckled with red. Steam rose in wispy white clouds. She should be cold because they were so high, but was not. The heat radiating up from Sid's body kept her from becoming an icicle.

"Why are you so warm?" She had to shout because she didn't think he could hear her otherwise.

It is the fire inside me.

"Ooh, can I see?" She'd seen his flame a few times but never got tired of it.

Not right now. It would bring too much attention to us. Also, you don't have to yell. You can speak to me just like I'm talking to you.

"How?" she shouted.

Humans are different than most animals. You have to concentrate to send out thought. Other animals have to train themselves to not project thought. If you think something deliberately and send it to me, I should be able to hear it. Try.

Aspen concentrated and sent him a *hey*, but he didn't react. She took a couple of deep breaths and thought about how he spoke to her. It always came like a voice, not a thought. And it never interrupted her thoughts, nor did she think he could read her mind. Very deliberately, as if she was speaking to him, she said, *Bet you thought I couldn't do it.*

He dropped a few feet suddenly, and she squealed and grasped his neck harder. *That was not very nice.* But she was smiling.

You think you are the only one who can tease. This is a much more efficient means of communication.

Yeah, why didn't you teach me this before?

I didn't think about it.

Tell me about the mark Skye gave you. Aspen's eyes started to water from the wind, so she buried her face in his neck. His scales were smooth and soft.

Like I said before, it's old magic. During the dragon wars, many different dragons were vying for leadership. Everyone wanted to be in charge, but no one would follow anyone. There was an ancient spell that would end it all. If one dragon could gain loyalty from all eight dragon races, well, nine at that time, then they would be king, and everyone would recognize him as their king. They'd have no choice. He'd reign for five hundred years with his own council. No one would be able to kill him or overthrow him. The magic made it impossible.

Every race wanted to be in charge, so gaining support from all the races was next to impossible. But there was a royal dragon who was loved by all. He eventually was able to secure loyalty from all the races.

That doesn't sound so difficult.

By swearing allegiance, they are giving their life. If I die, so do they.

How do they die?

It's a consequence of the sealing. If I were to die, they'd all die at the same moment.

Aspen's grip on his neck tightened. *So Skye basically gave her life to you.*

Yes. It was her idea. She learned how to invoke the magic when she learned how to remove her sealing. We're lucky she came to stay.

Is Skye the leader of her race?

No.

Then how come she could do it?

Because any dragon can speak for his race.

Aspen rested her head on the back of his neck. She was glad he found a way to save his life, but she felt like there was still something missing from his story.

Can you tell me more about the whole queen thing? I know you are trying to prevent it with this marking thing, but I'd like to know more about how things are supposed to work.

Sid dropped several hundred feet into a canyon, and Aspen gasped. *Sorry, it's not as windy down here. The process of choosing a queen is a secret. I will not understand it until I witness it. I do know that I don't have a choice and that the council chooses a queen because she exhibits qualities of*

an effective queen. A king is only as strong as his queen. It is very import-
ant that a proper queen is chosen, or it gives space for possible war. A weak
queen means a weak king, and those with a thirst for power would go after
the throne. We haven't warred in thousands of years. Dragons are typically
peaceful creatures.

Right now, a council of dragons makes all the decisions. It consists of one
dragon from each race. There are eight dragon races. Since the wars, the king
is always a royal dragon. Male royal dragons are gold, and female royal
dragons are silver. We live here in Yellowstone. The other races live all over
the world. Though each race has a presence somewhere in America. But only
since the wars. It wasn't always that way.

Obsidian was following a river. From that height, Aspen couldn't
tell where they were. A drop-off appeared ahead. He flew downward,
following a waterfall. Aspen felt the spray of water on her face. Just
before they plunged into the pool, he pulled up, and she realized they
were in the middle of the grand canyon of Yellowstone. The walls rose
sharply on either side of them.

Aspen's mind was reeling from the information about the queen.
She had no idea it was so complex. She'd ruined whatever chance Sid
had at having a normal reign, but for some reason she couldn't bring
herself to feel guilty.

You said there are eight dragon races. I thought there were only seven.
Red dragons from Hawaii, blue ones in Florida, orange in Arizona, yellow
in Texas, and white in Alaska. Oh, and those purple and green ones in Cal-
ifornia. Why do they have purple bodies and green wings when the other
dragons are all a solid color?

Legend has it that there were once two additional dragon races. One fully
purple who lived in the mountains and another fully green who lived in the
forests. When a dragon mates with one of a different race, that dragon will
have the body color of their mother and wing color of their father. It is said
that the dragons of the mountains and the dragons of the forests were very
fond of each other. After the wars, only the children survived. They are called
the woodland dragons, and they are very useful; they have healing powers.

Healing powers?

Obsidian didn't answer, but he soared around a mountain and flew into a wide cave. *You ready to meet another dragon?*

Hell yeah.

He landed inside the cave and let out an enormous flame. *His name is Damien.*

Aspen grinned. *What kind of a dragon is he?*

Fire, from Hawaii.

What's he doing here?

He was banished from his home. Skye and I used to visit him. He's a good friend of mine.

Obsidian crept down a tunnel, and blackness enveloped them. Eventually, Aspen saw a light ahead. The tunnel gave way to large cavern bathed in red light. In the middle of the cave sat the sorriest looking dragon she'd ever seen. His jaw no longer aligned. One eye was missing. Scars across his belly oozed with pus and blood. Almost all of his tail was gone, and his wings were in tatters.

Aspen slid off Obsidian's back and walked up to the disfigured dragon. "Are you Damien?"

Yes, and who are you, human?

I am Aspen.

Damien looked at Obsidian. He was quite a bit smaller than the king. About the size of her jeep, but with a long neck. Aspen bounced in place, itching to get her hands on the new dragon. He and Obsidian looked at each other for a while, and Aspen's patience wore thin. She knew they were talking, and it irked her to not be a part of the conversation.

"What happened to you?" she asked. He jerked his head down to look at her.

I lost my temper one too many times. A deep growl came from his throat, and he looked back at Obsidian. She knew he was irritated at being interrupted, but she did not like being left out.

She tapped him on the knee. He brought his head down again and bared his teeth at her.

"Would it be alright if I examined your body?" she asked, unfazed by his threats.

Why? he asked, irate. She didn't care.

"Because, you're a dragon, and I've only ever really seen Obsidian. I want to see if you are any different."

He jerked his head back to Sid. They were talking in their heads, and that pissed her off. She wanted to be part of their conversation. Finally, she decided she was done waiting for permission. Damien's wing was riddled with holes and tears. She tentatively brushed her fingers along a rip, and he shivered. He shook his wing, and her finger got stuck in one of the holes. He growled and brought his face back toward hers.

What do you think you are doing?

"I wanted to see what it felt like."

She untangled her fingers from his wing and moved around behind him. He followed her with his eyes. She placed her hand on the flat of his tail. The skin there was smooth, like the rest of his body.

She trailed her fingers along his scales, and although he followed her with those black eyes of his, he didn't complain. As she came around his front, she accidentally ran her fingers through the pus on his underbelly. She sniffed at it and wiped it on her jeans. She supposed she should be grossed out, but she'd seen loads worse.

She moved back around to his right side. She wanted to study his sealing. Surrounding his right ankle was a mark like hers, but it was a deeper shade of red than his body. She couldn't read most of the words, but the name stood out. Hestia.

Her heart ached for this poor dragon. Obsidian always seemed so powerful and indestructible. She never realized they could be hurt. She sat on the floor in front of Damien and motioned him toward herself with her hands. Damien lay down on the floor and rested his head in her lap.

You have a very gentle touch, he said.

"Thank you. How did you become so mangled?"

It's a long story.

"I don't think Sid and I are going anywhere anytime soon. I'd like to hear your story."

No one has ever asked me that before. I suppose it begins when I was a young dragon. I was charming and irresistible to females. Of course most of us are, being from fire. When other tribes send ambassadors to us, they never send females, and when we visit them, they hide their unsealed daughters.

A group of royal dragons came to visit us. This was an unusually large group. Whole families. One family brought along their daughter. She was about fifty years younger than me. The only females I'd ever been around were fire.

To me, she was a challenge. Something different. But she was also beautiful in a way that my sisters and cousins were not. Her name was Athena. I stalked the group and waited for her to be alone, for surely she wanted to explore our beautiful islands. My waiting paid off, and late into the night she flew off on her own.

I followed and convinced her to visit another island with me. We did not return to the Big Island for weeks. She captivated me and my heart. I sealed myself to her. Do you understand what that means for us?

"Yes, I do. But she didn't seal herself to you."

How do you know that?

"The marking on your ankle does not say Athena. It says Hestia."

Obsidian's educated you well. You are correct. She did not seal herself to me. I could charm and sweet talk her, and while she enjoyed my company, she did not fall in love with me. When we returned to the Big Island, her father was livid.

We don't typically mate with those not of our tribe. The royals are particularly sensitive about it. He hid her in the midst of their group and would not let me see her. In my arrogance, I tried to force my way into the middle. I thought if I could get to her, she would learn to love me and stay with me forever. I needed to be with her.

Her father fought me, which must've been horrid for him. It is not in our nature to fight one another, but he felt he was protecting his child. He was larger than me and a better fighter. I did not give up until he removed my tail in desperation. The group left after that. I wanted to die. I tried to, but Hestia, my friend and eventual companion, would not let me.

Hestia healed my stump and taught me to fly again. At first, my balance was off, and I would end up flat in the dirt. She stayed with me for years while my bitterness waned. She loved me, and I learned to let go of my love for Athena. Hestia and I were bonded and soon found that we were to be parents.

While we waited for the egg to hatch, Hestia grew ill. She was so weak that she could not fly. Our son was born, and she could barely open her eyes to gaze upon him. My family and I took her to the woodlands to see if they could heal her.

They tried. I know they did, but in the end it wasn't enough. After several months, she died. By then my family had all returned to the islands, and only my son and I were among the woodlands to mourn her. My fury at her death was horrid. I took out my anger on the woodlands. I fought six of them at once. I believe I killed one of them. My jaw was broken in the process.

I took my son and flew home. The woodlands must have sent a messenger to the leaders of my tribe because when I arrived, they were waiting. They claimed that I was not allowed to raise my son, that I would be an unfit parent.

I held him next to my stomach and protected him with my wings. The scars on my underbelly are from his claws when they tore him from me. They banned me from the islands, and I have not seen my son nor my beautiful home in five hundred years.

His story made his physical wounds seem trivial. Aspen longed to comfort him, to make him better.

"Obsidian?" Aspen asked.

Yes.

"If you live through this and are made king, will it be within your power to bring Damien's son to him?"

Of course.

"And will you?"

Yes, I'd do it even if he can't help me. Damien, why did you never tell me that story? Skye and I have been here loads of time to visit you.

Because you never asked, Obsidian. You and Skye were more interested in talking about yourselves. And while I enjoyed the company and your stories, you never asked about mine.

Old friend, I'm sorry. I'll not make that mistake again. But now we need your help.

Damien moved his head from Aspen's lap and looked at Obsidian. They spoke to each other, but included Aspen in the conversation. She wondered how they did that.

Aspen and I are sealed to each other. Sid stood very still as he spoke.

Damien coughed, and a small red flame escaped. He swung his head around and stared at the marking on Obsidian's ankle.

Nin Bereth, but that means...

I know what it means, Damien. I need your help to keep both of us alive.

Damien walked away and sat in the middle of the cave and stretched his neck out. She made her way to him and leaned against his neck. She wrapped one arm around him. Aspen couldn't help herself. She liked this poor dragon. He sighed.

Sid moved in front of him. *Do you see this mark?*

Damien lifted his head and stared at the mark Skye had given him. His body tensed underneath Aspen. *You fool, do you understand what you've done?*

I know exactly what I've done. Will you represent the fire dragons?

I'll be giving up my life.

No, you won't. I'm going to win this thing.

Damien stood up, and Aspen scrambled away. He snorted red puffs of smoke and narrowed his eyes at Sid.

After everything I've been through, I can't believe you'd do this to me.

Sid towered over him. *Do you want to see your son again? I'm your only possibility of that happening. I need your loyalty. Will you give that to me?*

Damien paced back and forth in the cave. He huffed and puffed, and every once in a while, he brought his head down and stared at Aspen. Finally he spoke again.

I don't agree with this. You undermine our whole system. All to save your own neck.

Sid held his head high.

I'm doing it to prevent the wars. If I succeed, then no wars will break out. But if I die and the wrong dragon is named king, we'll have a mess on our hands.

Damien narrowed his eyes at him. *You speak as if there is treachery within the potential kings.*

Possibly. Damien, I don't know who else to ask. You are my best chance at getting a fire dragon. Please.

Damien shivered, and then his whole body seemed to relax. *For the record, I don't agree with this. But I'll do it.*

Sid let out a breath. *Thank you, old friend, you won't regret this.*

Sid lowered his head, and Damien stared down at him. For a second Aspen realized what kind of danger Sid put himself in when he asked for their loyalty. He was in a very vulnerable position. With one quick movement, Damien could bite his head off.

Obsidian, on behalf of the fire dragons, I pledge our loyalty to you and only you.

Damien put his snout on Sid's head. Aspen watched as a red mark appeared on Sid's chest.

Aspen's head spun. She had no idea what they were talking about. And she knew better than to question Sid. He never answered a single important question. But Skye might.

CHAPTER II

THAT NIGHT ASPEN arrived at Sid's house ready to confront Skye. She'd wait until the boys went downstairs, and then she'd figure out once and for all what everything meant and what Skye's role was. Aspen knew they were keeping something from her, and she was determined to find out what it was.

Sid met her at the door with a big kiss, and for a minute she forgot what it was she was angry about.

"I can't do that when I'm a dragon," Sid whispered in her ear. Rowan brushed past them.

"I'm so tired of the PDA. Seriously."

Aspen giggled.

They entered the kitchen and found Skye elbow deep in some chocolate concoction. Sid put his arm around Aspen's shoulder and nuzzled her neck.

"Someday, I'm going to have something like that. You guys make me so jealous," Skye said.

Rowan coughed, and Aspen almost said something about someone being ready for the job, but restrained herself. Rowan would kill her if he knew she'd told Skye he liked her.

"Your birthday's coming up this weekend, right?" Skye asked.

Aspen nodded. She'd never been big on birthdays, but she'd never been opposed to celebrations either.

"We should have a party," Sid said. "It's a long weekend because of Thanksgiving. We can do something Friday afternoon."

"The last party was kind of a fiasco. Why don't we just have a small friends and family thing?" Aspen asked.

"Okay. Let's do Saturday night instead. Invite your parents."

"What time?"

Before Sid could answer, he was interrupted by the doorbell ringing.

Sid jumped up to answer the door. Aspen settled on a stool, and Rowan climbed onto the one next to her.

"Obsidian, son, what the devil are you doing?"

Rowan looked at Aspen with wide eyes.

"Dad, my name is Sid."

After that both voices dropped, and Aspen figured Sid was telling his dad that there was a human in the house that didn't know about dragons.

"Did that man just call Sid, Obsidian?"

Aspen shrugged. "What would make you think that?"

"He did. I know he said Obsidian."

Skye spoke sweetly. "Rowan, hon, we have no idea what you are talking about."

Rowan shook his head. "I swear I heard…"

Aspen hoped he wouldn't dwell on this. A few minutes later Sid came into the room, followed by a very tall and muscular dark skinned man with curly black hair that was cut close to his head. Covering his face was a bushy black beard. He was the type of guy that looked like he could break your hand with a simple handshake.

Skye wiped her hands and flew to him.

"Apollo," she squealed and flung herself at him. He chuckled and returned her hug, engulfing her.

She pulled away. "I've missed you. How are you?"

"Not good," he grumbled with a look at Sid.

Skye looked back and forth between them both and turned to Rowan.

"Do you want to go out to dinner, just the two of us?"

Rowan jumped off the stool so fast that he nearly fell over. Apollo caught him. Rowan adjusted his glasses, jerked his arm out of Apollo's grasp, and straightened his shirt.

"Sure," he said with a shrug and headed toward the front door. Aspen gave Skye a grin, but Skye grimaced. She was just doing this to get Rowan out of the house.

They left the room with Rowan talking animatedly to Skye. The rest of them didn't move until the front door slammed. Then Apollo turned to Aspen.

"Are you Aspen?" he asked with a growl.

She got off the stool and approached him. He didn't scare her. She held out her hand, hoping he wouldn't actually break her fingers.

"It's nice to meet you, sir."

He looked at her hand for a half second before he pulled her into a bone-crushing hug.

He let her go and held her at arm's lengths. "She's pretty, son, for a human."

Aspen wasn't sure what to think of him. She couldn't tell if he liked her or not.

Sid moved closer to her and slid his arm around her waist. "Yes, she is. I love her very much."

Apollo rubbed his hand over his head. "I figured as much. Let's sit. You need to tell me all about this mess you're in."

They sat at the breakfast table. Sid kept Aspen close, and Apollo sat across from them.

"Who told you?" Sid asked.

"Does it matter?"

"Of course it does."

"Why?"

"Because I need to know how much you know."

"Damien came to visit me right after you left him. Good thing your mother wasn't home."

"Why?"

"Well, for one thing, you know how much she hates him. For another, she'd kill Aspen for what she did to you. Can I see your mark?"

Sid moved around by his father and pulled his sock down so his dad could see the mark on his ankle. Apollo chuckled. "I was talking about the other one, but that's a nice one too." He looked at Aspen. "I bet you were shocked when a mark showed up on your ankle."

"Yeah, especially since I didn't actually know Sid at the time."

Apollo creased his eyebrows at her. "What do you mean?"

"My mark showed up when I met Sid on the mountainside as a dragon."

Apollo shook his head. "I don't know much about sealings, but from what I understand, it's rare for humans to seal themselves to dragons unless the dragon seals first. Humans fall in love so quickly and easily that there would be a hell of a lot of people running around with marks from unrequited love from a dragon during his human years. Aspen's the first human I've heard of who's sealed herself to a dragon. Well, except for Olivia, but that was expected. Come to think of it, I'm pretty sure her sealing came later."

"Who's Olivia?" Aspen asked.

"A story for another night." Sid whipped off his shirt. Aspen sucked in a breath. She still had not gotten used to seeing him like that.

Apollo stared at his son's chest, but for an entirely different reason than Aspen. He studied both the bright blue mark from Skye and the deep red one from Damien.

"Good, you only have two."

Sid scowled. "Why is that good?"

"Because I wanted to make sure Theo or your sister hadn't gotten to you first. Your mother and I believe in you, and I want to be the one to swear my allegiance to you."

"You'll have to go into hiding. I can't ask that of you. Theo's a better choice. I just haven't had a chance to ask him yet."

"Nonsense. I'm your father, and I want it to be me. I'm retired anyway. Hiding won't be a problem."

"What about Mom?"

"What about her?" Apollo raised his eyebrows at Sid.

"Won't she be upset?"

"She'd be angrier if she found out about it later, and I wasn't the one from the royal dragons."

"You do know what you are risking?"

"Of course I do. Why are you trying to talk me out of this?"

"Because I don't want you to die."

"You're assuming you won't make it. I daresay that young lady over there thinks differently. Now let's get this over with, and then I want to get to know Aspen a little bit better before I go home."

Aspen followed them out into the lawn and watched the same scene she'd seen with Damien. This time a brilliant gold mark appeared in the middle of Sid's chest. Aspen wondered what the words meant in the circle around the name.

Afterwards they gathered in the theater room. Apollo seemed to fill the whole couch. His presence was a little intimidating.

"Tell me about the first time you met my son. As a dragon."

Aspen told him about how Sid had dropped down in front of her, and she'd first gazed into those gorgeous blue eyes of his.

"Why didn't you run? Humans are terrified of us."

"I like dragons. Always have. I take pictures of them."

He stroked his beard. "You are an unusual one, aren't you?"

Aspen chuckled. "You're not the first one to tell me that."

He shrugged. "Olivia was too."

"Who's Olivia?" Her name kept coming up.

Sid pinched the bridge of his nose. "Dad will you stop bringing up Olivia? She was completely different than Aspen."

"Was?" Aspen asked.

"She's dead. Look, Dad, I need help. Who should I go to for the rest? I have three markings. I need five more, and the sooner I get this done, the easier things will be."

"You should go to Jolantha first. I'll come with you. You know the river and underground dragons better than I do. Canyon and arctic will be the most difficult. Do you think Candide will do it?"

Sid shrugged. "Unlikely, but I don't know any others. Maybe Jolantha knows someone. That or whatever canyon dragon we get. I know a few that might swear allegiance to me."

"I'll come back in a few days, and we'll go visit Jolantha. I need to get home to your mother and explain these new developments. We'll need to keep her away from Aspen until she calms down."

Aspen raised her eyebrows. "Is she really that scary?"

Apollo chuckled as he stood up. "You have no idea. Usually she's not, but she's a little protective of her son. The first time she met Skye, she nearly bit off her tail."

CHAPTER 12

ON SATURDAY MORNING, Aspen's parents met her in the kitchen. It was still dark outside. That was one thing Aspen hated about the winter, it seemed like it was dark all the time.

"There's my birthday girl," said Mom.

"Yeah, eighteen, crazy, huh? I bet there were times you didn't think I would survive."

Mom laughed. "Yeah, but you made it. What time do we need to be at Sid's?"

"About six. They have a chef coming in or something to make dinner. Skye's making the cake."

Mom finished her coffee and looked up at Dad. "I suppose we should go."

"Short shift today," he said and raised his mug to Aspen. "Happy birthday, baby. Tell Rowan we said so too. He's still asleep."

Aspen knew she should be excited for today. She'd been waiting years to be eighteen, but she was more excited about tomorrow. She, Sid, and Apollo were going to visit Jolantha, and Aspen was going to meet Sid's mom for the first time. Everyone seemed to think she should be terrified of her, but Aspen wasn't. Not much anyway.

Aspen poured herself a bowl of cereal and sat down on the couch to watch Saturday morning cartoons. She hadn't done this in years, but she was heading to Sid's in a few hours, and that wasn't enough time to go outside and do anything else.

Forty-five minutes later Rowan plopped himself on the seat next to Aspen.

"Since when do you watch television?"

"Since I turned eighteen. Happy birthday, bro."

"You too. You think I can get Skye to kiss me today? That'd make a pretty sweet birthday present."

Aspen snorted and muted the TV. "No, I don't. How many times do I have to tell you, she only likes you as a friend?"

He frowned. "We went out to dinner a few nights ago."

"Because Sid's dad showed up, and she wanted to get your nosy ass out of there."

A look of hurt crossed over Rowan's face, but he recovered quickly. "Whatever, we had a good time."

Aspen turned on the couch and faced Rowan.

"Skye doesn't have very many friends. You're probably the closest one she has because I spend too much time with Sid. Don't ruin that by trying to turn it into something it's not."

He sighed and crossed his arms. He didn't say anything else, and Aspen hoped he got the hint. Skye had been through a lot with Sid, and she didn't want to see her getting involved with yet another guy that she couldn't really be with. If Rowan made any moves, both he and Skye would get hurt.

A few hours later, Aspen and Rowan let themselves into Sid's house. They didn't bother to knock anymore and headed straight for the kitchen. Skye stood next to the KitchenAid and watched the batter carefully. Sid tried to stick his finger in it, and Skye swatted his hand away.

He looked up, gathered Aspen in a hug, and planted a quick kiss on her lips.

"Happy birthday, sweetie."

"Thanks. How's the cake coming along?"

Skye shook her head. "He won't keep his hands out of it. Take him away, please."

Aspen wiggled her eyebrows at Sid. "Gladly."

He laughed. "You know, tonight when your parents are here, we're going to have to go back to being friends."

Aspen scowled. "I know. But that's not any different than at school. Though I'm not used to it here at your house."

Aspen's phone buzzed. She reached around and pulled it out of her pocket. It was the reporter she turned all her dragon pictures over to. Weird, what did he want?

"Hello," she said as Sid and Rowan descended on Skye. They both stuck their fingers in the bowl, and she squealed.

The reporter's gravelly voice came out of the phone. "Hey, I wanted to be the first one to talk to you. I figured you owed me as much given all the restrictions you put on the photos you gave us."

"Excuse me, what are you talking about?"

"You haven't heard?"

"Heard what?"

"Early this morning a camera was recovered from a fella doing a documentary on the birds in Yellowstone. A massive golden dragon ate him. Same one that got that Dufour woman."

"Are you sure? Maybe it was a hoax. There are people who'd do anything to bring the dragons down. You saw the pictures I got of the dragons killing the one who was eating people."

"I'm certain of it. Saw the footage myself. There is no mistaking it. Now, would you mind answering a few questions for me?"

"Has the video already been released?"

"Yep, I'm sure you can find it on any local station. The park's shutting down until the dragon is found and killed."

Aspen's heart clenched. "Do they have a plan?"

"No idea, the announcement was just made. Now, can I ask you a few questions?"

"No." Aspen hung up the phone.

Sid was at her side in a second. "What's the matter?"

"The news, we need to turn on the news."

Skye produced a remote and turned on the TV by the table.

"No reports yet on what authorities are going to do about the dragon killing, but only authorized personnel will be allowed in and out of the park."

Behind the newscaster played a video. A man was attempting to get close to a bald eagle when a mass of gold appeared in front of the camera. When the mass disappeared, the man was gone, and the eagle flew away.

Aspen turned to Sid with her eyes wide. She didn't know what to say. She wanted to ask if he recognized the dragon, but she couldn't with Rowan there.

"Aspen, you okay?" Rowan asked. "I know how much you love the dragons."

"We need to go home, find out what Mom and Dad know."

Rowan nodded.

Aspen turned to Sid. "I'll call you later." Then she took out her phone and sent him a text. *I'm going to drop Rowan off at home, and then I'll be back.*

Sid nodded, and she flew out of the room, Rowan on her heels.

"I need you to grill Mom and Dad for me, can you do that?"

"Sure, are you going to see Obsidian?"

Aspen nodded. "He'll know what's going on and how to fix it. Will you tell Mom that I'm at Sid's house? Tell her you weren't feeling well or something."

"Sure thing." He grabbed her hand. "Hey, this is all going to be okay."

"I hope so."

As soon as they arrived, Rowan jumped out of the car. Her parent's car was still gone, but she figured they'd be home soon to check on them. Anytime the park got shut down, they came home to lay down new ground rules.

Aspen spun out of the driveway and sped all the way back to Sid's house. She found Sid, Skye, Theo, and Pearl in the living room. Pearl was the last person she wanted to see.

"What's she doing here?" Pearl asked with a sneer.

"Just because Sid and I broke up doesn't mean I don't care about the dragons. Besides, Skye is my friend." Aspen sat next to Skye and waited for someone to say something, but they were all quiet.

"Any idea who it is?" Aspen finally asked.

"No," Sid replied. "The section of the dragon we saw on the film could've been just about any dragon. If the camera had gotten his face, we'd be having a different conversation right now. I thought for sure Marc was the one."

"Well, he wasn't," Pearl said. "We have to fix this and fast. If we don't, we'll have another problem like we did in the seventies."

"What happened in the seventies?" Aspen asked.

"Nothing good." Theo chuckled. Pearl glared at him and turned to Aspen.

"There have always been those who wanted to slay the dragons. Every once in a while, a human would get lucky. Like George the Dragon Slayer, but he only got the small ones. They are mostly unsuccessful. However, in the forties a weapon was developed that would take out any creature, including us."

Aspen thought back to her world history course. The forties was World War II. Her stomach fell when she remembered what happened during the war.

"The nuclear bomb?"

Pearl nodded.

"How do you know this?"

"There was a family of dragons that lived near the first test of the bomb. They found their carcasses in a crater. Not only do they have a weapon that will kill us, but they know it will."

"That would involve bombing all the national parks. That doesn't seem logical at all."

"No, just this one. The other seven dragon races aren't killing anyone. Plus, they don't know how else to kill us. Humans feed on fear. If they don't understand how it works, they'll want to squash it. Bombs now are more sophisticated too. They could target just this park and not affect the surrounding towns."

"But aren't people afraid of the backlash?"

"We don't know. We haven't been in touch yet. We have ambassadors on the way, though, to talk to both the government officials in DC and those who manage the park here. We'll see what they say. This isn't good."

"You've said that already," said Sid.

"If they just shut down the park, then they they'll take away his food source," Aspen said.

"But what if he leaves?" Pearl asked.

"He'll be easier to track. You guys surely have a way you can find him," Aspen replied.

"We had every tracker out there looking for him before and no one found him," Pearl said.

Sid sat up suddenly. "The eagles. They will know who it is."

CHAPTER 13

S ID RAN OUTSIDE and whistled. He had no idea how to
fix this. He whistled again, and Bavol floated down from the
trees. He had replaced Talbot, and Sid wasn't as fond of him.

Yes, Your Majesty. He bowed and waited. Sid heard the door open
and saw Aspen coming outside.

Sid turned again and addressed the eagle.

*A human was eaten. One of you saw him. Find that eagle and bring
him to me.*

Are you certain, Your Majesty?

Yes. There was a video. In the background there was an eagle. Find him.

Right away, sir, I'll come back as soon as I have him.

Sid watched Bavol fly away, and Aspen approached.

"That was pretty amazing. Were you talking to him?"

"He's my messenger bird. He'll find the one on the video. It's our
best hope for averting a massacre." Sid was nervous. He'd been anxious
before, but this was different. This death made things worse. Even if

they did find and kill the dragon, the humans weren't likely to believe they'd gotten him, because of Marc.

"Sid, is there any way I can go with your ambassadors when they meet with the human officials? I have experience with both humans and dragons, and I might be able to provide insight no one else can." Aspen stared at him with a hopeful expression.

"Maybe. These meetings take place in Washington, DC. They meet with the president. I might have to go to this one."

"I'm sure we can find a reason to have me go with you."

"Let's see what the government decides first and what our ambassadors are saying. Also, we need to see what Bavol comes back with. I expect him to return before daylight tomorrow."

CHAPTER 14

WHEN ASPEN ARRIVED home, she found Rowan arguing with her parents. That was a sight she never thought she'd see.

"What's the matter?" Aspen asked, approaching the scene carefully.

Dad glared at her. "What have you done to him?"

She took a couple of steps back. Her dad wasn't usually angry with her. "Excuse me? I have no idea what you are talking about."

"This latest death is enough. Your mom and I have put in for a transfer. We don't want either of you around here."

"You can't do that. We're halfway through our senior year. We need to stay here. What does that have to do with Rowan?" Aspen looked over at her brother. He clenched his fists, his face red.

"He said the reason we can't leave is because you need to help save the dragons. I don't want you anywhere near those beasts."

Aspen and Rowan shouted at once, which was a good thing because then they couldn't tell exactly what choice names Aspen was calling them.

Both her parents stopped talking and waited while Aspen and Rowan finished their tirade. Aspen was glad she had Rowan to back her up.

"Are you done?" Dad asked.

"That depends on what you say next." Aspen crossed her arms.

"We've already booked flights to Hawaii. Sissy will get you enrolled in a school there. You leave tomorrow night. I don't want to risk you going off and doing something stupid."

Aspen smirked. "I hope you didn't pay too much for those flights."

Dad clenched his fists. "We're your parents. You'll go whether you want to or not."

"Did you forget that our birthday was today? We're eighteen. We don't have to go anywhere we don't want to."

"You will if you want our support. You're both getting on that plane tomorrow."

"Well then, I guess I'll go pack. Rowan you want to join me?"

Rowan looked at her with a frown.

Dad looked relieved. "Thank you, Aspen. We'll join you in a few weeks."

Aspen laughed to deflect the panic that was rising in her chest. Her father was being completely unreasonable. "No, I don't think you understand. I'm not going to Hawaii. I'll move in with Sid until you decide it's safe for me to move home. I'm sure he'll be happy to put up Rowan as well."

"Yeah, I'm going with Aspen." Of course he was. Especially if that meant he would be closer to Skye. Aspen stared at her parents for a minute, daring them to contradict her.

Mom looked like she was about to cry. "Can't you see? We just want you to be safe."

"Mom, how many pictures do I have of the dragons?" Aspen knew her parents were worried about them, but she couldn't move to Hawaii. She was in far too deep.

"That's not the point. You took those pictures before a dragon started eating people. You are more likely to get killed than anyone." A few tears leaked out of her mom's eyes.

"What if I promise to not go out taking pictures?"

"We've heard those promises before. I know you went out when we took your keys last time."

Aspen ran a hand through her hair. "Yeah, that was before I realized the danger. I have no plans of going anywhere that could get me killed."

Both Mom and Dad sat down. Dad put his arm around Mom's shoulder, and they looked at each for a long few seconds.

"Sissy's will be safer," Dad finally said.

"We're not leaving, so either we are staying here with you, or we're going to stay at Sid's house. He lives far enough outside of the park that we won't be in danger."

Dad shook his head. "I don't think so, Aspen. This is serious. You don't understand."

"I understand way more than you think I do. We spend a ton of time over there already. Not much will change. We just won't come back into the park. You guys can join us for dinner every night. Hell, you can even come stay if you want."

"You haven't even asked him yet."

"He'll say yes, trust me. Do you want me to ask him if he can open a room for you too? That way, we'll all be together, and Rowan and I don't have to go live with Sissy."

Mom let out a big sigh. "Your dad and I have to stay here. I'm still not sure about this. Will his parents be okay with you two living there?"

"He lives with his brother. His girlfriend lives there with him. His parents are out of the country." She had to fudge the bit about Theo. She didn't know how else to explain Theo and Sid's relationship.

Mom opened and closed her mouth. "I thought you were his girl-friend."

"I told you we broke up."

"I know, but you've spent so much time there, I just assumed you'd gotten back together."

"No. We're friends." Aspen knew she was wearing them down.

Mom let out a long breath. "I would much rather you go to Hawaii, but you're right. We can't force you. You'll be safer at Sid's than here. I don't want you in the park."

"Of course. I'll call Sid and make sure it's okay."

Mom gave Aspen a tight smile as she picked up the phone.

Sid answered on the first ring.

"Aspen? You okay?"

"Yeah, but my mom doesn't want Rowan and I staying in the park right now. Can we come stay with you for a few weeks?"

"You know you don't have to ask, right?"

"Well, my mom, you know, she wanted me to make sure it's okay."

"Yeah, sure. I'll open up a room for Rowan."

"What about me?"

"You'll stay in my room. Now pack a bag and get your gorgeous self down here."

Aspen looked at her mom, nerves setting in. She and Sid had never spent a night together except when they were camping, and that didn't count. What were his expectations? Aspen set her phone down on the table and wiped her palms on her jeans.

"Sid said it was fine. He's going to open rooms for both me and Rowan."

Her mom nodded, but still looked concerned. Aspen looked down at Rowan who was furiously typing on his phone. She kicked his shoe. "Come on, we need to pack."

He jerked his head up. "What? Oh, yeah, I'm coming."

Rowan followed her up the stairs to her room. He tripped over the last step, and Aspen looked back and saw him staring at his phone.

"Who are you talking to?" Aspen asked.

"Sid."

That was not the answer Aspen expected. "Why?"

"I told him I want a room next to Skye."

Aspen laughed out loud. "I admire your tenacity, brother, but you are fighting a losing battle."

He stopped and glared at Aspen. "I've fought a lot of losing battles. Trust me when I say, this is one battle I'm winning."

Aspen shook her head. When did Rowan grow a backbone?

Once in her room, Aspen dug her suitcase out from under her bed. It still smelled like the beach from Hawaii. She packed a few outfits and opened her pajama drawer. She would be spending the night with Sid. What did he expect? What did she expect? They had next to no alone time, so sex had never really been on the table. Was she ready to take the next step with him?

Who was she kidding? Every time he touched her, she wanted more. Even if sex didn't happen tonight, it would sometime. She packed a few tanks and shorts and then dug around the bottom and grabbed the box of condoms Sissy had given her before going to college.

She took a deep breath. She was ready for this.

CHAPTER 15

SID'S HOUSEKEEPER HAD gone home, so he and Skye made up the bed for Rowan. In the room right next to Skye's. Sid grinned. Rowan was in over his head, but he wasn't about to ruin the poor kid's dream. Skye seemed completely clueless though, so maybe Rowan had a chance.

Skye sat down on the bed and frowned at Sid. "If their parents are sending them here, they must be pretty worried."

"Yeah, I expect most humans are. Any ideas who it could be?"

"No. That's the worst part, right? We have no plan to solve this."

Sid sat next to her, and she leaned into him.

"Did I do the right thing with Marcellus? We all assumed he was the one doing it, but he tried to tell me it wasn't him, and I didn't listen. I shouldn't have killed him."

Skye put her hand on his knee. "He still deserved to die. What he did to Aspen is unforgivable. It was the right thing to do."

"I acted rashly and emotionally. I shouldn't have." Sid had been second-guessing himself a lot lately.

"You can't question your decision. You acted like the king. Not all the decisions you make will be the right ones, but you have to have confidence in your abilities, or no one else will."

"Skye, I think you will be my closest advisor should I make it out of this alive."

"I'd be offended if I wasn't. Wisdom is one of my best qualities."

Sid laughed. "That it is. Though I imagine Rowan has other ideas of what your best qualities are."

She grimaced. "First Aspen and now you. Do you really think he likes me that much?"

"I'd be surprised if there isn't a mark around his ankle."

"That's silly. He's just infatuated. He'll get over it."

They heard the front door open, and Sid raced down to welcome them. He grabbed Aspen's bag and motioned for Rowan to follow him. Skye waited at the top of the stairs.

"Can you show Rowan to his room? It's late. Aspen and I are going to bed."

Skye nodded. As soon as the door clicked shut, Sid dropped Aspen's bag and pulled her close and kissed her. He doubted he'd ever get tired of kissing her. It was the best part of being human.

She pulled away. "So this is new, huh?" She smiled, but it didn't reach her eyes.

"You mean that I get to spend the entire night with you in my arms, yeah. I don't know if I'll let you go back to your parents after this."

Aspen shrugged, and he checked her feelings. She was excited but scared.

"What's the matter?"

"Nothing." She ran her fingers through her hair.

"I can read your feelings. You're scared."

She glared at him. "That's not fair. But yeah, I'm nervous. We've never slept together before."

"We've fallen asleep plenty of times."

"Those weren't on purpose. We're about to go to sleep and wake up tomorrow morning in the same bed."

"I know. We're going to get used to this. Go change."

She went into the bathroom, and Sid stripped down to a t-shirt and his boxers. He couldn't stand to sleep in anything else. He slid underneath the covers and tried to figure out why she was so nervous. There was no reason for her to be. This wasn't that much different than anything they'd done before.

She stepped out of the bathroom wearing a tank top and short athletic shorts. Sid's breath caught. Maybe he shouldn't have been so quick to judge her anxiety. Suddenly, he felt self-conscious.

She slipped into bed with him and looked up with those gorgeous green eyes of hers. He kissed her so he didn't have to think about what it meant to have her here with him. She returned the kiss and leaned into him, laying her hand on his bare stomach. She dug her fingers into his abs, and he pulled her tight against him. He couldn't get enough of her. He flipped her over and relished the feel of her whole body underneath him. His fingers gripped her hair and held her head close to his, never letting her lips leave his.

He opened his eyes and gazed into hers. She smiled, and he felt her anxiety spike.

"There are condoms in my bag."

"What do we need those for?" Sid asked, confused.

Her fingers trailed up his back, and he forgot for a moment his question.

"You know I love you, but I'm not having unprotected sex with you."

Sid stopped and rolled off her. "I'm sorry if I led you on, but we aren't having sex."

Aspen creased her eyebrows. "I don't understand."

He chuckled and pulled her close to him again. "Dragons mate for life."

Her uneasiness disappeared. "I thought you'd never be able to be with anyone else anyway."

"That may be so, but mating only happens after we are bonded."

"How is that any different than being sealed?"

"It's how we become two halves of a whole. A bonding connects two dragons so they are literally the same soul. I don't know how else to describe it. However unlikely it will be, someday, I hope we can be bonded."

"But you're a dragon, and I'm a human."

"Stranger things have happened. Have hope, Aspen. I do."

She nodded and leaned up and kissed him again, this time with only desire and love, no fear.

CHAPTER 16

ASPEN WOKE THE next morning and found herself sprawled out across Sid's chest. She grinned. That was exactly where she belonged. She slid her hand up his t-shirt and rested it on his abs. He was so unbelievably hot. She couldn't quite believe it sometimes when she looked at him. She stared at his face. His eyes opened, and he watched her.

She leaned up and gave him a quick peck on the lips.

"Yep. You're stuck here. No going back to your parents' place even when it is safe."

"Not sure they'll go for that, but you can try."

"Hey, I have something for you." He leaned over the side of his bed and pulled out a small wrapped box.

"What's this?"

"Happy birthday. Yesterday got kind of ruined."

Aspen propped herself up on her elbows and unwrapped the box. Inside sat a black ring. It was the shape of a dragon, where the tail met the head, but the dragon's jaws were wide open and nestled in his teeth was a brilliant sapphire stone.

"Sid, it's gorgeous." The detail work on the ring was amazing.

The door to the bedroom flew open, and Aspen jerked around, dropping the ring. Pearl stood there with murder in her eyes.

"You have ten seconds to explain to me what the hell is going on."

Aspen sat up, ready for a fight. "What do you think?"

"I think you are trying get my brother killed." Pearl's eyes flicked to Sid's ankle, which was sticking out from under the covers. Her face went pale. "I guess it's a little too late for that. You little bitch, do you realize what you've done?"

Aspen jumped out of bed. "You have no idea what you are talking about. Besides, we have a plan to keep him alive."

Sid climbed out of bed. "Aspen, can you leave us alone? We have some talking to do."

Aspen crossed her arms. She wasn't going anywhere.

"No, she should hear this. After all, you've signed both of your death warrants. Who else knows?" She flung back her red hair and waited for a response.

"Skye, Theo, and Dad."

"Really, you told Dad?" Pearl rolled her eyes. "Whatever, get Skye and Theo and meet in the theater room in fifteen minutes. I can't wait to hear this awesome plan you have to save your life." Her words dripped with sarcasm.

She stormed out of the room, and Aspen grabbed Sid's hand. "I'm sorry."

"It was inevitable. Crappy timing, but still inevitable."

Sid dug around one of his dresser drawers and pulled out a pair of basketball shorts. Aspen found a pair of sweats and a hoodie. It was freezing. She brushed her teeth and went to wake up Skye. Sid was going after Theo.

Of course Skye looked just as good with no makeup as she did with. Aspen frowned at the sheer unfairness of it all. She shook her awake.

Skye blinked at her. "What's up?"

"Pearl is here. She knows about me and Sid."

Her eyes widened. "Oh, I'm in so much trouble."

"Yeah, but not as much as me. Get dressed and meet us in the theater room."

Skye nodded.

Aspen found Sid in the kitchen.

"Theo's not in his room." He drummed his fingers on the counter.

"Did he stay at Ella's?" Aspen put her arm around his waist, wanting to be close to him.

"If he did, he didn't say anything."

The front door slammed, and Theo skulked into the kitchen.

"What's everyone doing up so early?"

"Pearl's here. She found out about me and Aspen."

Theo gave them a wicked grin. "Uh oh, someone's in trouble."

"You're not off the hook. She wants to talk to all of us," Sid said.

Theo scowled but followed them to the theater room.

Pearl stood there with a frown on her face. She didn't say anything as they all filed into the room.

She paced and glowered at them. After what seemed like ages, she spoke.

"How long ago did this happen?"

Sid answered. "When I sealed myself to her, the marking already had her name on it."

Pearl creased her eyebrows. "I thought she hated you."

Aspen laughed. "I did. I got the marking when I met him as a dragon during the summer."

"When?" Pearl looked from one to the other. Her eyebrows creased.

"It was the day I became king. I landed near her on the mountain."

"Why did you do that?"

"Because I wanted to see a human up close. I wasn't thinking."

Pearl snorted. "That doesn't explain Aspen's marking. How long did you spend there?"

"A minute at the most."

"Sealings don't work like that," Skye interjected. Aspen looked over at her. Maybe she'd finally learn something Sid seemed intent on keeping from her.

"Could it be because she's human?" asked Pearl.

Skye shrugged. "Maybe. But nothing about how it happened with either her or Sid makes sense."

Pearl turned her attention to Theo. "Did you know?"

"Yeah. Sid wouldn't have pursued her otherwise. He's an idiot but not that big of one."

Pearl sank onto the couch. "Let's hear this plan of yours to keep you two alive, because I can't see any way out of this."

Sid sat down next to Pearl. "What I'm about to tell you is a big deal. I need you to swear you won't say a word to anyone else. If the council finds out about this, I'm a dead dragon."

Skye scowled. "You're already a dead dragon."

"No. I'm not. Not if this works."

Pearl sat back against the couch. "What on earth could you do that would…" She stood and backed away from Sid. "Please don't tell me you…"

"This was the only way." He pulled off his shirt, and Pearl stared at the marks on his chest. Aspen grinned at the sight. Again.

Pearl backed in the wall and covered her mouth. "This is treason."

"I'm the king."

"Not yet." She studied the marks for a second. "Not only have you sentenced yourself to death, but you've also made sure Skye, Damien, and…and…Dad. How could you do this?"

"Because I'm the king. I shouldn't answer to anyone, let alone a stupid council. Now, are you going to keep my secret or ensure my execution?"

Her face softened a little. "Of course. I don't want you to die, but…" She laid her hands on top of his marks. "But I hope you know what you're doing. Otherwise you're going to leave me without my brother and father. How long do you think you'll need?"

"I'm not sure. I'm hoping only a few weeks, but if the canyon and arctic dragons refuse, it could take a few months."

"That means I'll have to carry on like nothing is wrong. That includes continuing the search for a queen."

"Seems silly, but you're right. We're going to see about the woodland dragons today. Mom and Dad are coming with us."

Aspen jerked around. "Are you sure about that? Don't we need to find the human killer first?"

"Unfortunately, this can't wait. But this is two-fold. My father is the best tracker alive. He retired a few years ago, but this is important enough to pull him back into the game. They'll come with us to see Jolantha, and then he can start searching for the murderous dragon."

Pearl spoke up. "Well then, you better get going. The sooner you round up enough dragons to support you, the better chance you have of this working out."

Theo stood up. "I'm bushed. I'll see you this afternoon. That is if Aspen survives the visit to your folks." He winked and left the room.

CHAPTER 17

CAN I BRING my camera?" Aspen asked.

"Why?" Sid wondered why she would think of that in a moment like this.

"Because I haven't been close to many dragons, and today I get to see two royal dragons and a woodland one. Seriously. This is an awesome opportunity."

Aspen would someday be the death of herself. Sid shook his head at her. Skye and Theo weren't far off. Sid's mother would be furious with her.

"Let's leave the camera here. But we need to go. I want Dad searching for this dragon, and he needs to help us do this first."

Aspen followed him out the front door. He stopped dead when he saw what was on the front porch. Two eagles, both dead. Bavol and another Sid didn't know.

Aspen recoiled. "What happened?"

Sid reached down and fingered Bavol's feathers. "It looks like his neck was snapped. They saw something they weren't supposed to. What's bad about this is that whoever did this also wanted to send a message to me. We've got to get rid of this dragon. Wait here."

Sid spun and headed back into the house. He took the stairs two at a time and flung open Theo's door. Theo froze just before climbing into bed.

"Did you see any dragons when you were coming home?"

Theo shook his head and pulled his blanket up around him as he lay down. "Why?"

"Because the eagles I had out searching for him are on the front stairs, dead. It had to happen between the time you came home and now. That wasn't much time."

Theo frowned. "I came in the side door though, so they could've been there already."

"Dammit. I was hoping maybe you'd seen something."

"Sorry, but when I get up, I'll check the surveillance cameras and see what I can find. I'd do it now, but I'm exhausted, and I'll probably miss something. I'll have it done by the time you get back."

"I didn't think of that. I've never looked at the cameras before. Don't worry about it. I'll check it myself."

"No, dude, you've got bigger things to do. Your dad is the best at what he does. He can find that dragon. You go talk to him, and I'll check the cameras. If we find anything on them, then we can update your dad."

Sid nodded. Theo was right, he should get going.

He found Aspen and Skye outside with the dead birds.

"We should give them a dragon's requiem. They died serving you," Skye said and wrung her hands.

"We should." Sid turned to face Aspen. "You are about to witness a dragon's requiem. No pictures."

Aspen nodded. "Is that what you did for Marc?"

Sid shook his head. "It's similar, but we never finished it with him. He didn't deserve the respect."

They placed the eagles out in the middle of the field.

"I'll take Bavol. You take the other one."

Both Sid and Skye transformed. Sid let Skye go first. Her silvery blue flames covered the tiny eagle, and seconds later Sid's black flames engulfed Bavol. Then they both let out their flames at the same time, and the ash was gone. Skye transformed back and walked to the middle of the field to pick up two gemstones.

"What's that?" Aspen asked.

"We make gems out of their ashes." She held one out so Aspen could see the gigantic diamond-like gem streaked with brown.

"The stones typically take the color of the dragon. I've never seen one for eagles."

Come on, Aspen, let's go. We need to get this over with so my dad can go out searching for this bastard.

Aspen jogged away from Skye and scrambled onto Sid's back. They took off into the biting wind.

CHAPTER 18

ASPEN WASN'T GOING to lie. She was scared of Sid's mom thanks to Skye. She hung tightly to Sid's neck as he flew into the mountains and straight into a cave. Aspen had no idea where they were. The cave was wide, and they flew deep into the mountain. It smelled of still water and sulfur. Fires lit the way. Eventually Sid landed and changed into his human form.

"It would be better if we were all human during this discussion."

"You mean so your mom doesn't bite off my head."

Sid squeezed her hand and gave her a tight smile. "Yeah, something like that."

At the end of a long hall they found two enormous dragons, one gold and one silver, both asleep. Their scales glittered with the light of the fire in the surprisingly warm room. Aspen unbuttoned her coat, and Sid followed suit.

"It's their body heat. Once they change to human, it will cool down quickly."

He placed his hand on his father's flank and pushed against him. It didn't even move the dragon.

Sid laughed. "Heavy sleeper. I've never tried to do this as a human."

He moved around and tickled his dad's nose. The dragon snuffed and two puffs of gold smoke floated out.

His eyelid cracked open, and Sid moved around and waved at his dad.

"Good morning."

Apollo rose up on his haunches and then nudged the silver dragon.

She sat up, and Aspen could've sworn she saw a grin form. Within seconds they both changed into human. Sid's mother looked just like Pearl. She gave Sid a big hug, and Apollo embraced Aspen. He smelled woodsy like Sid. "It's so good to see you."

"Thanks."

Aspen turned and faced Sid's mom. She stalked toward Aspen with a glare. The smile she had given Sid had disappeared. Before Aspen knew what happened, the woman slapped her across the cheek. Hard. Aspen's eyes watered as she brought her hand up to her face.

"Mom!" Sid said and rushed to Aspen's side.

"This girl has ruined everything." Her voice shook, and her face flushed red.

Apollo approached her. "Athena, dear, calm down."

Athena spun and faced him. "No, I will not. If it weren't for her, everything would be okay, but now both of you are going to die. It. Is. All. Her. Fault."

The name Athena niggled something in Aspen's brain, but she couldn't figure out what. She decided to try to apologize. Winning this woman over would be in her best interest.

"I'm sorry. I didn't mean for any of this to happen. I'm just trying to make the best of things right now."

Athena crossed her arms. "We should kill you right now."

"You know that won't change anything. I'll still be executed," Sid interjected.

"Do you have any idea what you've done? Even if you manage to secure the loyalty circle, you'll open us up to war, and you'll be weak because you can't be bonded to anyone but the queen. It's suicide either way. I can't believe you're going to sacrifice yourself over a stupid girl."

"I can love Aspen and still be an effective king. I know I won't have the strength of the other kings who could take on their queen's power as well, but I will reign. Completing the circle guarantees that."

"If it weren't for her, you wouldn't need the circle. You're going to get killed, and you've dragged your father into this too."

Apollo put his hand on Athena's arm. "I did that of my own choice. Sid didn't even have to ask. Now, son, why don't you show your mother who else you have?"

Sid pulled off his shirt, then tugged on Aspen's hand so she was standing right next to him. Sid pointed at each mark on his chest.

"Skye, Dad, and Damien. They all did this for us. Not me. Us."

Athena crossed her arms and eyed Damien's mark. Aspen gasped.

"I know where I've heard your name before. You and Damien were a thing before you met Apollo."

Sid shook his head, and Athena rounded on Aspen, eyes blazing and red hair flying in every direction. "Listen here, you little brat, you have no idea what my life has been like. I don't want to hear a word about what you know or don't know. You'll learn a lot more if you keep your mouth shut. I can't believe my son fell in love with an insolent child like you."

Sid opened his mouth, but Apollo cut him off. "That is in the past. Aspen couldn't know how hard that was for you. Now, Sid, I've told your mother that we're going to go out and see Jolantha today. Are you ready to go?"

"Not exactly. There's been a complication."

Athena sniffed. "That's probably *her* fault too."

"Mother, please. Could you at least try to be nice?"

She pursed her lips. "No."

Aspen saw Sid roll his eyes. "Whatever, we still need your help. Dad, we thought we got the human killer, but he's still out there, and he's killing again. We've got ambassadors trying to smooth things over in DC, but this has gotten out of hand. Can you track him?"

"Your father is done tracking dangerous dragons. Why don't you just have the eagles do it?" Athena asked.

"I did. They came back dead."

Athena covered her mouth, and Apollo stroked his beard. His face betrayed no emotion.

"Your dad can't go after a monster like that. He'll get hurt. Do you remember what happened on his last mission?"

"Of course I do, but I don't know who else to ask. We had trackers out before, and no one has even gotten close to him. Dad, you're the best."

"Now, not only did you make sure that he dies if you die, but you want to send him out on some suicide mission to track a dragon that is probably the most dangerous one we've had in several hundred years."

"Now, Athena, I've searched for more dangerous dragons, and nothing ever happened to me. Yes, I know we had that scare on my last mission, but that was a long time ago. Besides, this dragon hasn't hurt any dragons."

"That we know of. I don't like this."

"I'll be more careful this time. I'd be honored to serve you, son. I'll head out this afternoon. Maybe you could show me places we know he's been."

"I don't like this," Athena repeated.

"Dad will be fine. We can build a team to go with him if that will make you feel better."

"Nonsense, I work better on my own. Besides, I can't very well build a team when I have a mark on my chest that says I no longer recognize the council."

Sid took a deep breath. "Yeah, you're right. Let's go see Jolantha. Then you can come home with us, and I can take you out and show you what we know about the human killer."

Athena's face hardened. "I hope you know that we're doing this for you, not for that thing." She nodded toward Aspen.

Sid pulled Aspen close, but kept his eyes trained on his mother. "What you do for me, you do for her. Let's go."

CHAPTER 19

GETTING JOLANTHA'S SUPPORT was easier than Sid thought it would be. They'd arrived home fifteen minutes ago, and Aspen collapsed on Sid's bed.

"I'm exhausted. Your mom really was as bad as they said. I thought everyone was exaggerating."

"She'll come around. She has to. But it's a good thing we won't see much of her."

Aspen giggled and patted the bed. "Come here. I want to see your new mark."

Sid sat next to her. "You're just trying to get me to take my shirt off."

She shrugged. "Maybe. Though, I have to admit, every time you whip your shirt off, I get a little dizzy."

Sid gave her a crooked grin. "Yeah, good to know."

"Just don't do it while I'm driving."

She grabbed the sides of his shirt and tugged. Her boldness shocked him, and if he was being honest with himself, made him lose all thoughts of dragon wars and gathering supporters.

Her fingers brushed his skin, and he shivered. She scooted closer to him and pulled his shirt up farther.

"Arms up," she said as if she were talking to a small child. Sid complied, still a little taken aback by her nerve.

He didn't say anything as she studied each of the marks.

"I like Jolantha's the best. The blend of purple and green is gorgeous. What do the words around the name mean?"

"There isn't an exact translation, but it's something like loyalty to the king forever."

"Do you still speak this language?"

"No. Our language evolved much like the human language did, but I have a dictionary on the shelf."

She nodded, and he hoped she wouldn't ask about their own tattoos. He didn't want her to know what the one on his ankle said.

Aspen shifted a little and traced her fingers along the other marks, muttering the names.

"Jolantha, Damien, Apollo, and Skye. Why is Skye's pure blue if she's part royal dragon?" She looked up at him with those wide green eyes, and instead of answering her, he leaned down and kissed her.

"You're trying to distract me." She giggled and pushed him away.

"Who? Me?" He pulled her into his lap. "Actually, I was the one who got distracted. I can't even remember what you asked."

She laid her head on his shoulder. "I was wondering why Skye's mark is only blue."

"Oh, yeah. It's because her father was a sea dragon. She cannot speak for the royal dragons."

A knock sounded on the door.

"Come in," called Sid.

Theo poked his head in. "I checked the security cameras."

"What'd you find?"

"You'll want to see this."

Aspen handed him his shirt. "Shame, but I don't think Theo likes looking at that as much as I do. I'm going to see what Skye and Rowan are up to."

She slipped out of the room past Theo, and Sid put his shirt back on.

"Where's your dad? I thought he was coming back with you."

"He wanted to take my mom home. She's still pretty upset with him going out into the field. He'll be back in a couple of hours."

They entered a small room full of monitors that Sid had only been in a couple of times. He had no idea how it all worked. Theo sat down in front of the screens.

"Our system is pretty complex, so I wasn't prepared for this. Watch."

Theo hit a button. "I'm going back in time. Here is where you and Skye gave the eagles a requiem." Sid watched the scene unfold backwards, from the requiem to him and Aspen finding the dead eagles. Then the screen went black. Seconds later everything was back, but there were no eagles.

"What happened?"

"I'm not sure, but we literally lost an hour of footage. I checked all the cameras. Every single one goes black and comes back on an hour later."

"He'd have to have a pretty good knowledge of computers and security systems. That narrows the field a little bit."

"Yeah, it would have to be a dragon that's been human in the last thirty years. Before that the technology was quite different."

"True. We also have to look at the area. They probably live near Yellowstone because that is where all the deaths are occurring."

Sid crossed his arms. "That still leaves thirty or forty suspects. Who knew this would turn into such a big deal. We have to find him."

"He knows what he's doing. He's good at this. He knows we are looking for him, and he doesn't want to be found."

"My dad can find him."

"Let's hope so. We're dealing with a dangerous dragon. Are you sure you want to send your dad after him?"

Sid wiped his hand across his face. "I don't have any other choice."

He left Theo in the room with all the security cameras and went in search of Aspen. He figured she was in the kitchen, since that was where Skye spent most of her time.

Skye and Rowan were arguing about whether Skye should add walnuts to her brownies. Rowan held the bag of walnuts out of her reach. Aspen was across the room, watching them with a cute grin on her face.

"Brownies aren't meant to have anything in them." Rowan smiled down at Skye.

She stretched for the bag but wasn't even close. "But the recipe calls for them. I've never had brownies with walnuts. I might love them. Give them back." She jumped up, but Rowan backed up.

Aspen approached Rowan. "Come here, Skye, let me show you how this is done."

She tickled Rowan's ribs, and he brought his arms down and retreated from both girls. Aspen made a grab for the walnuts, but he raised them above his head again and glared at them.

"No walnuts."

Aspen turned to Skye. "He's all yours. Ribs and feet are his most ticklish, just so you know."

Footsteps pounded in the hall outside the kitchen, and Sid turned to see who it was. He could hear Rowan laughing and Skye squealing behind him. Inwardly, he was glad she was happy, but he worried about Rowan. Eventually Skye would have to leave.

Apollo entered the room, his face twisted in anger.

"What's up?" Sid asked.

"Your mother."

"She'll be fine. She's just worried about you."

Apollo snorted and motioned toward Aspen. "Oh, we argued about me going back out into the field, but mostly we fought about that one."

"Why?"

"She blames her for all of our problems. Whined about her all the way home. When I told her that I thought she was perfect for you, she stopped talking to me. Wouldn't even say goodbye when I left." Apollo crossed his arms and watched Rowan and Skye wrestling with the walnuts.

"Perfect for me, huh?"

Apollo smiled. "I'm not sure Pearl could've found you a better queen."

Sid scowled. "She will be my companion forever, but she won't be my queen."

"Why not?" Apollo asked.

The front door slammed, and Pearl came gliding into the room.

"Hi, Daddy," she said and pecked her father on the cheek.

"Hey, princess. Looks like you've been keeping a good eye on your brother."

"Bad eye you mean. Look at the mess he got himself into."

"Sid knows what he's doing. I have faith he'll live to his next birthday and several hundred after that."

"Let's hope so. But none of us are going to live until our next birthdays if this idiot dragon doesn't stop eating people."

"That's why I'm here. Let's get this show on the road."

"You be careful. Sid shouldn't have pulled you into this."

"I'll do whatever I need to serve my king."

Sid's stomach clenched. "You don't have to do this."

"Yes, I do. Honestly, I wish you had come to me when this all started. Then it wouldn't have escalated."

"I didn't want to bring you out of retirement for something we could handle."

"Well, I'm here now. A few more weeks then this will all be behind us."

Skye squealed, and suddenly walnuts rained down all around them.

Everyone turned to look. Both Rowan and Skye held one end of the walnut bag, which had split into two.

Rowan gave Skye a grin. "Looks like I win."

CHAPTER 20

ECEMBER CAME IN with a monster snowstorm, but in spite of the foot of snow that had fallen the night before, they still had school. Early Monday morning, Aspen, Sid, Rowan, and Skye piled into Sid's Escalade and slowly made their way into town.

Aspen was so sick of school, but it provided a normalcy to all the craziness. There, she didn't have to think about Sid risking his life because of her or the dragon terrorizing the park.

Just before they got out of the car, Skye spoke. "Hey, we need to stop at the store on the way home."

"How come?" Aspen asked.

"Because I need more walnuts." She opened the door and escaped out of the car before Rowan could retort.

Aspen met his eyes in the rearview mirror. "You're welcome."

"For what?"

"Like you didn't enjoy having her hands all over you yesterday."

Rowan shrugged, and Aspen giggled.

"Do you think she'll be mad when she finds out you prefer walnuts?"

Sid started laughing. "Really?"

"On top of brownies, not in them. But I didn't get a chance to explain that to her before things got out of hand."

Sid opened his door. "We need to go inside. School starts in two minutes."

Aspen groaned. "Three weeks until Christmas break. I can't wait."

They braved the snow, and stomped off their boots when they got inside. Tori was standing by a set of lockers near the door. She threw her arms around Aspen.

"I feel like I haven't seen you in forever."

"It was just Thanksgiving."

Tori shrugged. "Well, your party got cancelled because of that stupid dragon, and you ignored my texts."

"My phone died. I'm sorry."

Tori pouted for a second and then recovered. "We're planning a snowmobile trip this weekend. You up for it?"

"Where? The park's closed."

"We figured you could get us in."

"It's really dangerous right now. We should wait until the dragon is caught."

"When did you become a wuss?" Tori flung her hair over her shoulder and looked at Aspen expectantly.

"Did you forget that this dragon killed Matt, Lila, and Mrs. Dufour? This isn't a joke. No one should go into the park."

"You live in the park."

"Not right now, I don't. Rowan and I are staying at Sid's."

Tori raised her eyebrows. "Really? Figures you wouldn't tell me. I guess you two made up."

"It's complicated. I don't even know what we are right now." The bell rang, and they all ran for homeroom. Dufour had been pretty lenient about tardies, but Hudson was not.

The next two weeks flew by in a routine of school, work, and home. Every few days Aspen's parents would join them for dinner.

The dragon hadn't killed anyone else. At least not that they were aware of. Sid thought he was probably still eating people, but had gotten smarter about it.

Rowan still didn't know that he was living with a bunch of dragons. It was getting more and more difficult to distract him when Apollo showed up. Though, most of the time, Apollo simply flew over the house and gave Sid updates in his head.

A week before Christmas break, Aspen's parents brought Chinese takeout for everyone. Just as they started to eat, Apollo strolled into the room, looking pale. Sid jumped up.

"Dad, you okay?"

He nodded. "I'm just a little worn out. We need to talk." He looked around the table.

"Dad, this is Stacey and Jason. Aspen's parents."

Aspen's dad stood up. "I thought you were out of the country." He held his hand out. Apollo looked at the hand and then grinned at Aspen before he pulled her dad into a bear hug.

Aspen snorted. Dad would not like that. He barely hugged her. Apollo let go of him, and Dad straightened his shirt. "It's nice to meet you."

Apollo laughed. "You too. I've been dying to meet the parents of the girl who stole my son's heart."

Stacey looked from Aspen to Sid. "I thought you said you and Sid were just friends. That Skye was his girlfriend."

Aspen squirmed. "It's complicated."

"Did you lie to us?"

Skye, who was sitting next to her mom, laid a hand on hers. "Mrs. Winters, Sid and I had this on again off again thing. But in the last couple of weeks we realized it would never work, and Aspen and Sid have been sparking again."

"It's true." He sat down and ran his hands through his hair. "I'm totally in love with Aspen, and she still hasn't decided if she wants to be with me yet. But she knows how I feel about her."

Aspen was floored by how quickly Sid and Skye were able to make up a story. Apollo plopped down in the seat next to Aspen and put his arm around her shoulder and pulled her close.

"I, for one, hope she decides to get back together with my son. She's good for him."

Aspen's mom and dad exchanged a look, but before they could say anything, Sid spoke up.

"I wasn't expecting you, Dad."

"I'm only in town for a night or two. I'm getting too old for all this travel."

A look of concern passed over Sid's face, but Aspen knew he couldn't say anything as long as her parents were there.

The rest of dinner was awkward, and Aspen had never been so happy to see her parents leave. She walked them to the door.

Mom hovered in the entryway. "I'm not sure how I feel about this if you and Sid are getting back together. Maybe you should come home. There haven't been any more disappearances. They're talking about opening the park up for Christmas."

"We are safer here. Seriously."

"I don't like you living with your boyfriend."

"Mom, I'm eighteen."

"But still in high school."

Aspen resisted the urge to roll her eyes. "Sissy left home for college when she was seventeen. I'm not a child."

Rowan laughed, and Mom looked at him. Of course his eyes were glued on Skye.

"Rowan looks happy," Mom said.

"He has a thing for Skye."

Dad chuckled. "He sets his sights high."

"Yeah. But he is happier than I've ever seen him. He gets along well with Sid and Theo too. He works out with them every day."

Mom's eyes bugged. "Rowan?"

"Yeah, I know."

Dad pulled Aspen in for a hug. "We just worry about you guys. I'm glad you had someplace to go."

"I know. Maybe after Christmas we can come home."

"If they open the park up, I want you both back in your own beds."

Fat chance of convincing Sid of that, but she didn't say that to her mom. She just smiled and nodded.

As soon as Aspen closed the door, she went back in search of Sid and Apollo. Rowan and Skye were alone in the kitchen, loading the dishwasher. "Where'd they go?" Aspen asked.

Skye turned around. "Upstairs. Sid's putting Apollo in the room right next to yours."

Aspen made her way upstairs and found Apollo sprawled out on a bed and Sid sitting on a chair next to him. She sat on the edge of the bed. "What's up?"

"Dad was attacked by hawks today."

"Hawks?"

"Yeah, a swarm of them attacked him and basically shredded his wings. He was lucky he got here. I sent an eagle for Jolantha. She'll be able to heal the wings. For now, Dad, you should rest."

"Don't tell your mother."

Sid grinned. "I know. I didn't even tell Jolantha why I needed her, just that she needed to come. She should be here in the morning. Can I get you anything else?"

Apollo shook his head. "I just want to sleep."

"Of course. Come on, Aspen, let's leave him be."

As soon as they got back to their room, Aspen asked the question she didn't feel comfortable asking in front of Apollo.

"Why did the hawks attack him?"

Sid shrugged. "No idea. The eagles have always been loyal to us, but the hawks have never been terribly friendly. Though they've never attacked us before. This just gets weirder and weirder. I don't know what we're dealing with."

CHAPTER 21

T HE NEXT MORNING, Sid rolled over to find Aspen already out of bed. But her spot was still warm, so she couldn't have been gone long.

He peeked in his dad's room and saw he was still sleeping. Skye and Rowan were in the kitchen.

"Where's Aspen?"

"Out in the garage with Jolantha. She arrived about thirty minutes ago. Are you going to school today?"

"No. But Aspen should go. Her parents won't be too happy with us if she stops going to school."

Sid found the deep purple dragon curled up on the garage floor and Aspen leaning against her brilliant green wings. It was sweltering in there. Sid took off his coat and hat.

Jolantha swiveled her great violet head around. *Hello, Obsidian. Hello.*

"Good idea to bring her into the garage," he said to Aspen.

"It was better than standing out in the cold. Jolantha was telling me stories about before the purple and green dragons became one race."

"Sounds interesting. I'm going to go wake up my dad. Aspen, you need to go to school."

She sniffed. "Since when did you become my dad?"

"Since I want your dad to continue to let you stay here. You can drive the Escalade. I'm going to stay home and make sure my dad is okay." Sid looked at his phone. "You've got about thirty minutes."

Aspen sighed and stood up. "Will you still be here when I get home?" she asked Jolantha.

Jolantha gave her an answer that Sid couldn't hear, but it made Aspen frown.

"Well, come visit us again."

Aspen pecked Sid his cheek and went back into the house.

I like her. She's a good human to keep around, Jolantha said.

Yeah. She is.

Aspen wouldn't tell me why I'm here.

Apollo got hurt. I need you to heal him. Sid paused for a fraction of a second and then forged on. *And don't tell my mother.*

Jolantha snorted, and two purple puffs came out of her nose. *I expect your mother will find out anyway. But it won't be me who spills the beans. You should know I was in the middle of securing you a canyon dragon when your eagle found me.*

Sid jerked his head up. *What are you talking about?*

I have a few good friends down there. Some who are pretty anti-council. I was close to getting a commitment too.

Sid opened and closed his fists. He'd had Theo and Pearl searching for him, but neither had trusted any of the canyon dragons to even ask.

As soon as we finish up with my father, I'll head down there with you.

You should leave Aspen home for this one.

With any luck, we'll be there and back before she gets home from school. But she'll be pretty upset when she sees the new orange mark and she didn't get to go along.

Go get your father. Let's get this show on the road.

Apollo was already waiting in the kitchen when he returned. Skye, Rowan, and Aspen were all searching for backpacks and homework.

"Come on, Dad, let's get you patched up."

Apollo followed Sid out the back door as Aspen called goodbye. As soon as they got into the backyard, Apollo changed into a dragon. His golden wings were in tatters.

Sid's throat tightened. He felt like this was his fault. "They got you good."

Jolantha studied the wounds and then placed her snout on top of Apollo's head, and Sid watched as the wings knitted themselves back together. Within seconds she was done.

Apollo let out a deep breath.

"Dad, go home. We'll find another way. This isn't worth it."

No, this is personal now. I'm going to find this bastard.

"Look at what he did to you."

No, he didn't do this. He was too cowardly to face me himself.

"Be glad he didn't. You are not a warrior. You're a damn good tracker, but I don't want to risk your life. Seriously, go home."

No. I'll find him, and I'll be fine.

Sid ran a hand through his hair. His dad was being stubborn. "Then at least take Theo or Pearl with you. Please."

Son, I'll never find him if I have tag-a-longs. I'll be safe.

"You know Mom will never forgive me if something happens to you."

I know. But it won't. I promise I won't engage him in a fight. Once I know who he is, I'll come straight back to you.

Sid sighed. He wouldn't win this fight.

"Okay, but the second you even sense that something is wrong, you bail. Do you understand?"

Yes, Your Highness. Apollo flew off without even a backwards glance. Sid turned to Jolantha.

I should probably ride you. If the canyon dragons see a black dragon flying in their territory, they will be suspicious.

Jolantha dropped to ground, and he climbed on her back. The flight down to the Grand Canyon took about an hour. Jolantha landed near the edge of the park. *Wait here. I'll be back in a little bit.*

Sid nodded and changed into his dragon form. It was too cold to stay as a human. He curled up and waited. About thirty minutes later, Jolantha came back with an old orange dragon that Sid had never met.

He didn't even have a chance to introduce himself before the dragon spoke to him.

I'm not that old.

Sid hated talking with the canyon dragons. They could read all your thoughts, so they answered before you even got a question out. It was annoying.

If you don't want my help, why did you come?

It's not that I don't want your help, but I don't like my mind being read.

That's who we are. My name is Helios. Jolantha and I are old friends. Let me see your marks.

Sid stood taller so that Helios could study his marks.

You only have four.

I'll have a river dragon next week, and then I'm already planning a visit to the underground dragons.

And the arctic?

That was Sid's biggest fear. He worried that he wouldn't be able to secure their help. They were in charge before the dragon wars, and they wanted their power back.

It seems mighty risky for me to pledge myself to you when you cannot guarantee that you will win.

If I can guarantee I can win, can I count on your support?

But you can't. You know no arctic dragons. Did you forget I can read your thoughts?

You misread them. I know them. I just don't know who it will be yet that will help me.

I will need more than just a promise you can win. I also want to secure more territory for our race.

Excuse me?

We are not a peaceful race, and the canyonlands have become crowded. Food is scarce, and we'd like more territory.

Where?

I believe the woodlands have some southern territory they'd be willing to part with. Also we never see river dragons in their western territory.

So you are asking me to take lands away from other dragon races so that you can have more?

Yes.

Sid couldn't do that. Not without pissing off the other races. Jolantha's voice entered his head.

We'd be willing to share. Not give it to them completely, but allow them to hunt on our land. I imagine the river dragons would as well.

That would be fair, Helios said.

I would need to talk to the river dragons first.

The dragon cocked his head. *That is fine. But that doesn't fix the first problem.*

What problem is that?

You can't guarantee that you'll win. Don't bother to come see me again until you have seven seals on your chest. Then I'll provide the eighth.

He took off before Sid could say anything else.

That didn't go as planned, Sid said.

No, but you're closer. If you can secure the rest of them, you know he'll help you. I can work on him too. We're a little more than just friends.

Sid snorted. *Don't you get sick of him being able to read your thoughts all the time?*

Sometimes. But I got used to it. Go home. I'll let you know if I make any progress. In the meantime, get the rest of those seals. You need them.

CHAPTER 22

THE NEXT FEW weeks passed without much action. For which, they were all grateful. Friday afternoon Aspen ran to the car. "Christmas break," she said to Sid as he slid into the driver's seat. She gave him a kiss, and he grinned at her. "Two full weeks with no school."

Rowan and Skye climbed into the back. "We should do a movie marathon tonight," Rowan said.

"Sounds awesome. What do we want to watch?"

"*Star Wars*." Rowan took off his glasses and rubbed the bridge of his nose.

"No," said Aspen and Skye at the same time.

Aspen liked *Star Wars*, but she didn't want Rowan and Skye fighting again. All they did lately was bicker. Skye had tried to watch the first movie with Rowan a few weeks ago and fell asleep. Rowan didn't speak to her for two days. He couldn't fathom someone not loving *Star Wars*.

"How about *Lord of the Rings*?" Aspen suggested.

No one argued, so they stopped by the store to pick up junk food and then hit Little Caesars and bought six pizzas.

By the time they got home, it was after dark, and they found Pearl in the kitchen with a scowl on her face. "A park ranger was eaten today. We need to go to DC. The government is freaking out."

Aspen's stomach clenched. "Do you know who it was?"

"Not your parents. I checked. But I can't remember the name. The point is, we have to go."

Sid put his hand on Aspen's back. "Okay, Pearl, can you book three tickets to DC?"

"Three?"

"Aspen's coming."

She rolled her eyes. "Why?"

"Because she'll be beneficial in the meeting. Plus, I want to introduce her to a few of the underground dragons."

"Underground?" Aspen asked, confused.

"Yeah, they live in the caverns and spaces under the ground. They're tricky to find and don't come out very often, but I know where a few are near DC."

Aspen had never heard of the underground dragons. She couldn't wait to see them. Though the circumstances in which they were heading to DC were less than ideal.

Athena stormed into the room a minute later.

"Mom, what are you doing here?"

"I need to talk to your dad."

Aspen retreated, hoping Athena wouldn't see her.

"I haven't heard from him in a few days, but I'm sure he's fine. If he's hot on the trail, he won't take time out to let us know where he is," Sid said.

She creased her eyebrows. "I'm just worried. I also wasn't speaking to him when he left, and I want to make up with him."

"Do you want me to send an eagle if I hear from him?"

"That would be good, thanks, son."

"We gotta go to DC for a couple of days. Do you want to stay here?"

"No, I don't like being human. Send me an eagle when you get back, and let me know how things go."

CHAPTER 23

THE FOLLOWING MONDAY Aspen, Sid, and Pearl boarded a plane to DC. Aspen had no idea who they were meeting or what the outcome would be, but she was thrilled to see another dragon race.

They sat in first class so the flight didn't seem that long.

After the plane touched down, two people met them at the gate. Each gave a little bow. "Your Majesty."

Sid smiled at them. "No need to be formal. Just call me Sid. Everyone else does, and it will be awkward around those who don't know."

"I'm Aspen." She held out her hand, and the man grinned at her, displacing all his wrinkles.

"So I've heard. I'm pleased to meet the girl who has turned the dragon world on end."

Sid leaned forward. "Did Theo tell you?"

"Of course. I'm the one who told him to involve Pearl."

Sid turned to Aspen. "Jonathan is Theo's father. Who else knows?"

"I haven't told anyone, so it depends on who you've told."

"Now Raja knows," Sid said inclining his head to the man who had his arm around Pearl's shoulder. Aspen thought she recognized him.

"Raja already knew," Pearl said.

"This was supposed to be a secret."

"It can't remain a secret if you want all of us to support you," Raja said.

"And will you?" Sid asked.

"Of course," both Jonathan and Raja said at the same time.

"Where are we going?" Aspen asked.

"To the Pentagon. The meeting will be in an hour. Then you can head back to Montana," said Jonathan.

"Reschedule the flight for late tonight. I need to meet with Darneil."

Jonathan whistled. "Darneil doesn't like to be found."

"He likes me. We've been friends for a long time. Besides, I think he'll like Aspen."

"You're the one who takes all those pictures?" Jonathan asked.

"I am."

"Yeah, you're right. Darneil will like her."

They rode in a limo, and Aspen marveled at the opulence of it all. She wasn't sure if she could get used to the idea that this would probably be her life. They arrived at the Pentagon thirty minutes later, walked along a long hallway, and took an elevator several floors down. Everyone in the full room stood, and a few people gave a small bow. To Aspen's surprise the President of the United States stood at the head of the table. Sid took his place at the opposite end.

"Madam President," Sid said, inclining his head to her. She was a tall woman with short, severely cut brown hair.

"Your Majesty," she replied with a smile. "Please sit."

Aspen took the chair next to Sid, and the others sat at various points around the table.

"Allow me to introduce my military generals and their advisors."

The four men dressed in impeccable uniforms nodded as she introduced them one by one.

"Thank you for meeting with us today," Sid said.

"We don't want to make a decision this grave without consulting you," President Johnston said.

"Of course."

"We have a dragon who is killing people. We were told the situation was under control only to have another individual killed. Have you identified the dragon?"

"No, Madam President, we have not. We have every dragon trained in tracking looking for him. We will find him," said Sid.

"But what do we do in the meantime?"

"Let me do my job and find the dragon."

"I'm afraid that's not good enough. We need to let people know that we are tackling the problem." She whispered something to the man sitting next to her and then looked up at Sid again.

"If it makes you feel any better, bring in the military to make it look like you are doing something, but it will be more effective if you could just stay out of our way."

Aspen was surprised to hear him talk like that. He'd never sounded so in charge before.

"If I'm sending the National Guard, they will do more than just sit and look pretty. Surely they can assist you in your search and help with security."

Sid sighed. "Okay. They can keep an eye out for him. But every male dragon in Yellowstone is gold. It doesn't mean they are the killer."

Aspen couldn't tell for sure, but it looked like the president rolled her eyes. "I think our troops are more professional than that. They can tell one dragon from another."

Sid rubbed his forehead. "Sure. We can use them. Especially if it will help ease the public's mind."

The general sitting to the president's right spoke. "I'll contact the governor of Montana to bring in the Guard. You should also be aware of the plan if you do not resolve this issue promptly."

"What do you mean?" Sid asked.

"Let's say this dragon eats a few troops, and we can't find him. We need a resolution."

"Like what?"

The president answered instead of the general. "We have the resources to take out the dragons in Yellowstone without impacting the surrounding towns, and we will. This problem needs to be taken care of now."

Aspen couldn't take it anymore. "Excuse me, I don't understand. Does this mean you'll kill all the dragons if the *one* dragon that is eating people isn't found?"

"Only the ones in Yellowstone."

"You realize that's an entire race of dragons."

"That's irrelevant. When a herd of cows contracts mad cow, we'd kill the whole herd. This is the same thing," President Johnston replied.

"This is not the same thing, and you know it. This is not a disease, and we're not dealing with mere animals. How many known serial killers are out there right now?"

A man in the middle of the room answered. "Right now there are forty-two."

"Forty-two. Huh, that's a high number. Maybe we should nuke the towns they terrorize so that they can no longer kill anyone. How does that sound?"

"That's absurd," the president said.

"That's what you are proposing."

"People live in those towns."

Aspen stood, fuming. "Who do you think lives in Yellowstone?"

"Dragons." The president stared at Aspen.

"And you feel dragons are expendable."

"My job is to protect the *people*."

Aspen gestured toward Sid and the others. "What do they look like?"

The president went quiet for several seconds. "I never quite thought of it that way."

"I've spent a considerable amount of time with the dragons, and I believe they may be the more intelligent species. I wouldn't underestimate them. If Obsidian says he can take care of this dragon, then he will."

The president nodded. "I won't do anything rash without consulting with you again, but we will not take it off the table. Let's plan another meeting in four weeks if the problem isn't solved. Earlier if more people are killed."

Aspen was about to retort, but Sid cut her off. "We couldn't ask for more, Madam President. Thank you for meeting with us."

Sid stood, and everyone followed suit. He left the room first, followed by Aspen and the other dragons.

Jonathan put his hand on Aspen's back, leaned over, and whispered in her ear, "I've never seen anyone speak to the president in that manner before, and I have sat in too many meetings with her. You are a natural. When Theo told me what happened, I thought Sid was a dead man, but now I'm not so sure. He chose wisely."

He dropped back so he was walking with Raja, and Aspen flushed, unsure of how to take the compliment. When they exited the building, Sid reached back and took Aspen's hand. "You were phenomenal. Thank you. Now let's meet Darneil. He's going to love you."

They drove into a rather seedy part of DC, and Aspen locked the doors.

"Bring your good camera with."

"Okay." Aspen grabbed her backpack.

They stopped in front of a rundown brownstone. Sid looked at the others. "Come back in a couple hours?"

"Just send us a message when you are ready to go."

Sid stepped out and pulled Aspen with. Three men stood on the corner. Each of them had muscles the size of cantaloupes, baggy jeans, and scowls. Aspen clung to Sid's arm, but she wasn't sure even he would be able to protect her if one of those guys pulled a gun. The men looked at the car with a glint in their eyes, but before anyone could do anything, the car was gone.

Sid and Aspen walked up a set of crumbling stairs, and Sid knocked on the door.

A young woman dressed in a halter top and mini skirt appeared. "What do you want?"

"My name is Obsidian, and I'm here to see Darneil."

Her eyes widened. "Of course, Your Majesty, come in. I'm sorry I didn't recognize you." She waved them in, and Aspen was grateful to be in the house, though it didn't look much better on the inside. "Do you know the way, or do I need to show you?" the woman asked.

"I know the way." Sid pulled Aspen into the house and to a rickety stairwell. Aspen looked down. It went on forever.

"How far are we going?"

"All the way. It's about ten stories. The trek down isn't that bad, but going up is killer. I like to fly if I can."

"Um, you wouldn't fit in the stairwell."

"I wouldn't, but Darneil does."

"Why'd you ask me to bring my camera?"

"Darneil loves to show off. I'm surprised he hasn't called for you. Everyone knows you are the go to girl for dragon photos."

The walk down was terrifying. Aspen kept both hands tightly clasped on the handrails, even then she thought for sure her foot was going to go right through one of the rotted stairs.

They rested when they reached the bottom. Aspen inhaled the musty air and ran her fingers along the wet walls. The chilly air caused goose bumps to rise on her arms.

Sid opened a metal door and waved Aspen through. They entered a massive cavern. It took Aspen's eyes a few minutes to adjust because the room didn't have normal lights. The whole room shone an eerie blue. She looked down at her shoes. They glowed white. Paintings of tiny brightly colored dragons covered the walls.

"What's with the black light?"

"White light burns the underground dragon's eyes. Shame because they are gorgeous but can't come out. They used to be able to fly around at night before electricity. But now they are stuck inside. A few still exist in undeveloped areas, but you'd be surprised how far light pollution has spread. Besides, all it takes is one wayward flashlight, and they are blind. It's just safer for them to stay underground."

At first Aspen couldn't see anything, but as they walked deeper into the cave, she noticed colored shapes hanging near the ceiling next to all the black lights.

"What color are the underground dragons?"

"Brown, but they're chameleons, so they change color depending on their surroundings. They love it when others bring them scraps of fabric so they can try new colors."

As Aspen and Sid walked farther into the cave, she noticed mirrors winking along all the walls. At the end of the cave they found two dragons lounging on fancy pillows in front of two large mirrors. Both were multicolored and gorgeous. The one on the left was about the size of a ferret, and the one on the right was the size of a large cat. They were the tiniest dragons Aspen had seen. She was fascinated. She had always loved the river dragons and asked her mom if she could have one as a pet. If she had known they came smaller, she would've searched every cave near her home for them.

The smaller dragon lifted his head up when Sid approached. *Bless my eyes. Is that Obsidian I see?* Aspen was glad he projected his thoughts so she could hear them as well.

"It is indeed. How are you, Darneil?"

I'm doing well. It's been close to a hundred years since you've shown your ugly mug. What brings you here?

"You've heard the news that I'm the new king?"

Of course I heard. Best choice in my opinion. Don't do that thing where you make small talk before getting to the business at hand. Tell me why you're here.

Sid waved Aspen forward. "This is Aspen. She's the love of my life, and the council has a problem with that."

Darneil's body shook with laughter. *You do manage to find yourself in trouble, don't you? I don't understand what this has to do with me.*

Sid whipped off his shirt. "I'm asking for your support."

Darneil stuck his snout close to Sid's chest and studied each of the four seals.

You're asking me to pledge my loyalty to you?

"Yes."

I'm afraid I can't do that. But I'll keep your secret.

"Why not?"

I have my reasons. You won't find a single dragon in this cave who will give up their life for yours. But we should make the best of your visit. Now tell me more about this lovely lady.

Sid crossed his arms, and Aspen could tell he was trying to figure out what to do. "She photographs dragons. She has pictures of all of the dragon races except the underground. Would you like her to take your picture?"

Darneil started quivering. *I'd love it. But first, can she take pictures of my daughter?*

Darneil pointed with his wing to the larger dragon on the pillow next to him.

"Of course." Sid studied her for a second. "She's not a pure underground dragon though, right?"

"I beg your pardon?" The small dragon whipped her head around and glared at Sid. Aspen was startled to hear an actual voice.

"I didn't mean any offense, but based on your wings and your ability to speak, I'd guess your mother was a river dragon."

"She was, but I don't see how that is any business of yours."

Runa! Obsidian is the king. You will not speak to him that way. Apologize. Now.

"No," she said and stuck her tongue out at her father. Aspen immediately liked her.

I'm sorry for my daughter. She's young and insolent.

"Only because you keep me cooped up here. I want to go outside, stretch my wings."

"But what of your eyes. You'll go blind," Sid said.

"Nope. I tested it several years ago. I'm immune."

It's still dangerous.

"Whatever." She stood up and crawled across the pillow and stuck her snout right into Aspen's face. It took every ounce of courage Aspen had to not back away from her. But she didn't want the dragon thinking she was scared. Not that she was really scared, but she was startled by her closeness. "Do you really take pictures?"

"I do. Can I take yours?"

Runa nodded. Aspen reached into her bag and pulled out her camera. She turned off the flash and hoped she would still be able to get good pictures. The little dragon sat down and stretched her neck high. She spread out her wings, revealing a multicolored belly.

Aspen took a few shots. "Can you change the color of your wings too?"

"No." She scowled. "The yellow is the curse my mother left me. But she also gave me the ability to speak and to see outside, so it's not that bad."

"Can you turn around?"

Runa did as she was asked, and Aspen took several more shots.

"Can I see?" Runa asked.

"Sure." Aspen flipped through the pictures and showed them to her.

"They are good, but I want to see what I look like in the daylight."

Absolutely not. You aren't going anywhere. It is my turn now.

Darneil primed and posed for his pictures. After Aspen promised them that she would have pictures printed and delivered, they let her go, only to be assaulted by several other dragons who wanted their pictures as well. They were all gorgeous, and Aspen couldn't wait to see what the pictures revealed in the light of day. A couple of hours later, Sid touched her elbow.

"We need to go. We've got a flight to catch."

She picked up her backpack from the floor. It felt heavy for some reason, but that was probably because she hadn't been wearing it. She almost looked inside, but Sid was sprinting down the hall. What was his hurry?

Aspen ran after him.

"Come on, we can get a ride this way."

"I want to say goodbye to Darneil and Runa."

"We'll see them again soon. We have to. I need their support, but first I need to figure out why they wouldn't give it to me. Come on."

A couple of tiny brown dragons waited at the bottom of stairs. "Sorry, she was tied up with the pictures," said Sid.

One of the dragons rolled his eyes. They both opened their wings and hovered over Sid and Aspen.

"Grab his foot and hang on tight."

"He's a fraction of my size."

"Doesn't matter. He can still lift you. Just don't let go."

Aspen gripped the feet of the dragon as tight as she could, and within seconds she was flying. She didn't like this flight much. She'd much rather be on the back of a dragon.

The dragons deposited them on the top step and flew back downstairs carrying packages that had been left for them.

"Food," Obsidian explained.

"Who takes care of them?"

"A few of the royal ambassadors who live around DC. Taking a human form is beneficial in this situation."

"Why do they take care of them?"

"Because we take care of each other. All of us feel a sense of obligation to them. We don't want them to go extinct like the green and purple dragons did."

"But the green and purple dragons still exist."

"Not separately."

The ride back to the airport was long, and Aspen was exhausted by the time she got back onto the plane. She slept most of the way home.

It was early in the morning by the time they got back to the house. Aspen threw her backpack on the bed.

"Ouch," the bag said.

"What the?" Aspen asked, approaching the bag carefully.

She unzipped and a bright purple head poked out. "That's better. Where are we?"

"Runa, What are you doing here?" Aspen asked.

"Daddy wouldn't let me out of the cave otherwise. What was I supposed to do?"

CHAPTER 24

S ID WALKED INTO the room and froze when he saw Runa. "Your father is going to be furious. I'm sending you home." The dragon climbed all the way out of the bag. "No, please, keep me here. I've always wanted to see the outside. Don't make me go back there. Daddy will understand. Please. Just for a little while."

Sid grimaced. "I don't know. Let me send someone to talk to your father. You're too young to make these decisions on your own. Why didn't you just wait until you're of age?"

"That's twenty years. Twenty years rotting down in that cave. I saw my opportunity, and I took it."

Sid frowned and left the room. Runa lay down flush on Sid's bed, turning the deep blue of his bedspread. It was beautiful with the yellow wings.

"Do I look pretty?" she asked.

"Gorgeous," Aspen admitted. "How'd you get through the airport? Tell me I didn't send you through the x-ray machine."

"The ceiling was yellow. I flew over you and climbed back into your bag later. It wasn't that hard. The colors are magnificent." She hopped off the bed and turned the white of the rug on Sid's floor.

"Show me more."

Aspen nodded and the dragon flew to her shoulder and landed, gripping it tight. Aspen giggled and walked out of the room, watching the tiny dragon bob her head and change color every time they walked past another painting on the wall.

They entered the kitchen, and Rowan turned to look at them.

"Is that a dragon?" he asked.

"No, I'm a bat." Runa stuck her tongue out at Rowan, and he frowned.

"Runa, this is my brother, Rowan. He doesn't know much about dragons."

"No excuse." She flew off Aspen's shoulder and landed right in front of Rowan. She stuck her face in his, and he backed away. She moved closer, then she looked at Aspen. "You have the same eyes."

"A lot of people tell us that."

She got extremely close to Rowan's face again, and he blinked rapidly but didn't move away. Runa squeezed her eyes shut, and seconds later she peeked her eyes open. "Did I get it?"

"You did," Aspen responded to the brilliant green color.

"Picture, picture." Runa jumped up and down. As soon as Aspen snapped a few, Runa spoke again. "Lemme see."

Aspen showed her the screen. "Ooh, pretty. I think I like that color best. I'm keeping it for a while." She looked around the kitchen.

"Where's Obsidian?"

Aspen's eyes flashed to Rowan, who looked confused. "He's probably trying to smooth things over with your father. You're in a lot of trouble, missy."

"I'm not going back down there. You can't make me." Her head perked up when a bird flew by the window. "Is that the outside? Let's go."

She bounced up and down again like an excited toddler.

Aspen nodded and Rowan got up to follow her.

Runa jumped up on Aspen's shoulder again, and Aspen opened the door. It was cold, but the little dragon didn't even notice. She stretched her face to the rising sun and hopped onto the bare concrete of the patio. She spread her wings and flapped away.

"Don't go far," Aspen called.

Rowan stood next to Aspen. "Skye didn't seem surprised to see a dragon hopping around on the kitchen table."

"Yeah, I know."

"Can you explain?"

"You won't believe me."

"Try me."

Aspen sighed, knowing this wouldn't go over well. "You can't tell anyone."

"I won't. You know that."

"Sid is Obsidian's human form."

Rowan didn't say anything for a full thirty seconds, and then he busted out laughing. "You mean your boyfriend is a dragon?"

"Yeah, and not just any dragon either. The king."

Rowan ran a hand through his hair. "That's messed up."

"You're telling me. It's freezing out here. I hope she's almost done. Runa's not supposed to be here. She stowed away in my bag."

Rowan frowned. "So how does Sid know the others?"

"You mean Pearl, Skye, and Theo?"

"Yeah."

"Pearl is his sister, Theo is his best friend and mentor, and Skye was his girlfriend before he came here to be human."

Rowan paled. "You mean Skye is a dragon?"

"Yeah. She's got the prettiest silver wings I've ever seen."

"But, she seems so human." Rowan dug his hands into his pockets, and his shoulders slumped.

"They all do. Except Pearl. She's pretty intense and uptight. I'm surprised she didn't freak out when Runa hopped around on the table, but it's possible she doesn't know the implications. Runa's father hasn't let her out of their cave since she was born eighty years ago. From what I gathered, she snuck out once, but that didn't last long."

They watched her do loop de loops in the air. Her body became the bright white color of the snow, but she kept her head and neck green like Aspen's eyes. Then she sunk into a drift.

"What is this stuff?" Runa called from across the yard.

"Snow."

"How deep is it?"

"A couple feet."

She took off again and then dive bombed into a small mound. She laughed as she shook the snow off her wings.

"This is awesome. Now I've seen snow. Can I see the ocean?"

"It's not anywhere near here, but someday."

Sid came out of the house. He looked at Runa "What is she doing?"

"Playing in the snow. She's never seen it before. Did you get in touch with her father?"

"No. I have ambassadors on their way. They are going to call me when they have news. Darneil isn't going to be happy. Can you take a few pictures of her playing outside? Maybe I can send them, and if he sees her safe and having fun, he might let her stay for a little while."

"Can I use your phone? That way you can just send them from there?"

"Sure."

Aspen snapped a few of Runa jumping around in the snow and another one of her in flight chasing a blue jay. She'd turned the same blue and white that he was and looked incredible.

Sid sent the pictures and looked sidelong at Rowan. "What's his problem?"

Rowan wouldn't look at Sid. His arms were crossed, and he was shaking.

"I'm just cold," he said.

"I had to tell him about you. He knows you all are dragons now."

"Ah. I'm still Sid." Sid touched Rowan on his elbow.

Rowan kept his eyes trained on the ground. "No, you are the Dragon King. That's kind of a big deal." His face was screwed up. Aspen wished she knew what he was thinking.

"I'm still me," Sid said with a frown.

Rowan turned and stormed inside.

"He'll come around. He just needs to get used to the idea. It's freezing out here. Runa, come back inside. We're cold."

She landed in front of Aspen, spraying snow everywhere.

"Can I play outside later?"

Sid answered. "Sure, I might even go flying with you. But we aren't doing anything until we find out how angry your father is."

"We already know that. He's going to be even more angry than when I snuck out the first time."

"I don't know about that. At least now he knows you can't hurt your eyes. That was pretty stupid."

Runa glared at Sid and flew up to Aspen's shoulder. When they entered the kitchen, Skye was cooking bacon and eggs. She could make a decent breakfast, but dinner was still questionable.

Sid's phone buzzed, and he gave Aspen a tight smile. "The ambassadors in DC. Let's hope Darneil was reasonable. I'll be back in a few minutes." He disappeared out the door. Aspen figured he didn't want to talk in front of Runa.

"What do you eat?" Skye asked Runa.

"Chicken mostly. Sometimes pork or beef. Whatever the ambassadors bring us."

Skye held a piece of bacon for Runa.

"What's this?" Runa sniffed it.

"Bacon. Try it."

Runa snatched it out of Skye's hand, and as soon as she swallowed, started jumping up and down. "More."

"I have to cook, but maybe Rowan can feed you."

Rowan looked a little lost. Aspen pushed the plate of bacon in front of him. He tentatively picked up a piece and held it out for Runa.

She gobbled it right down and opened her mouth again. Theo started talking to Rowan about their workout routine, and Runa pushed her head against Rowan's cheek. He laughed and fed her another piece of bacon. Aspen let out a breath of relief. He wasn't too distraught over the "everyone's a dragon" thing.

Aspen helped Skye bring the food over. She'd gone all out. Bacon, eggs, sausage, fried potatoes, and pancakes.

Aspen sat next to Rowan, and Runa settled herself between them both, helping herself to whatever she wanted from either one of their plates.

When she took a chunk out of Rowan's pancake, he scolded her. "If you want something, ask. That was mine."

"Fine. I want a pancake."

He fed her a small piece, and she turned and snatched some scrambled eggs from Aspen's plate. "Bleck. I don't like those."

Aspen laughed. "I was beginning to think you'd eat anything."

Rowan held a sausage in front of her snout, and she grabbed it.

"Do you have a human form too?" he asked her.

"Nope. Only the royal dragons can do that. Aspen was right. You don't know much about us, do you?"

"Maybe you can educate me."

"I don't know that much either, except what my father taught me. He wasn't too interested in the outside world," said Runa.

Skye sat across from Aspen. "I can teach you both. You too, Aspen, if you want. History was my favorite subject. I had different lessons than Obsidian because I wasn't supposed to become a human."

Rowan's head snapped up. "What do you mean you weren't supposed to become human?"

"I'm only half a royal. My father was a sea dragon. I got my wings from my mother."

"So you are one of those blue dragons?"

"Yeah."

"Excuse me." Rowan pushed away from the table and escaped out of the kitchen.

"What's his problem?" asked Runa. "I wasn't done eating."

"I'll feed you," Aspen said. Guilt gnawed at her insides. She knew exactly what his problem was. Rowan went crazy while they lived in the Everglades, and he was terrified of dragons after that. Aspen guessed he saw something with a blue dragon, but he wouldn't tell her.

"When will you show me the ocean?" Runa asked Skye.

Skye gave her a tight smile. "Someday."

Sid came back into the room.

"I've spoken with the ambassadors for your father. He's furious. But he was pleased with the pictures we sent. He said you can stay for a few weeks, but then you have to go home."

Runa shook her head. "I'm not going back. Not ever. You can't make me."

"Runa. I need his support. You can stay for three weeks, and then I'm bringing you home. What you do after that is up to you, but you can't stay here. You're too young to make those decisions on your own."

"What do you need his support for? He can't give you another one of those marks."

Sid sat down next to her. "Why not?"

"Because all of the underground dragons already have a mark. They pledged their loyalty to him. If he pledged his loyalty to you and then you died, they would all die."

Aspen creased her eyebrows. "But I didn't see any marks."

"That's because we can hide them."

Aspen had forgotten the camouflage ability. They could all be marked, and no one would ever know.

"Do you have one?"

She shook her head. "I'll be the leader of the underground dragons when my father dies, so it is stupid for me to give him my loyalty. But this means I can give you my loyalty. I'm not tied to anyone."

Sid swallowed. "No. I can't ask you to do that. I'll find an underground dragon in one of the remote areas. I respect your father too much to accept that from you."

She stuck her tongue out at Sid and snatched another sausage off Aspen's plate.

"Hey, I thought Rowan told you to ask first."

"He's not here, is he?"

She ate half the food on the table and then toddled off down the hall.

"Where are you going?" Aspen asked.

"To find Rowan."

"I'll come with you."

Aspen knocked on his door.

"Come in," he called.

She pushed the door open. Rowan was lying on his bed, staring up at the ceiling. Runa jumped up, curled up next to him, and rested her head on his chest. She closed her eyes and within seconds was snoring.

Rowan chuckled. "She likes me."

"Almost as much as Skye."

"Why'd she have to be a dragon?" He pinched his lip and stared up at Aspen.

"Because she is. Nothing is going to change that."

"I almost could've lived with that. But she's one of those blue ones. I can't even…"

"What happened in Florida? And don't tell me nothing, because something happened, and it had to do with the sea dragons, or you wouldn't be freaking out."

"I don't want to talk about it."

"Maybe you should talk to Skye about it. She can probably help you with whatever issues you have."

"It hurts. You know. Right in my chest. I've never felt this way before. I always liked Tori, but I never really knew her, you know. But Skye, I'm totally in love with her."

"No, you're not. Trust me."

"How do you know?" He rubbed his eyes.

"Because dragon love is different. They mark you when you fall in love."

He sat up suddenly, and Runa grumbled, but resumed her nap next to him instead of on him.

"You mean like this." Rowan peeled his sock away. The familiar tattoo surrounded his ankle in a gorgeous silvery blue of loops and swirls. Her eyes widened.

"Yeah, like that." Aspen wasn't sure what to think of this development. She was sad that Skye would never feel the same way.

"I'd seen yours and Pearl's. I was terrified to say anything though because I didn't know what it meant. Skye can never know. I didn't know it was because of her."

"You should tell her."

Rowan squeezed his eyes shut. "No. Aspen, I can't do that. Please keep this secret for me."

"Of course. But you really should tell her."

"Why?"

"Because if she ever falls in love with you back, neither of you will ever be able to love another. How long have you had it?"

Rowan shrugged. "A few days."

Aspen whistled. "You have no idea what you've gotten yourself into."

"Come on, Runa, we're all going to bed." Aspen stood in the doorway of the theater room with Sid behind her.

"No, I don't want to. Skye's teaching me lessons."

"Sounds like she's just telling you stories."

Runa stuck her tongue out at Aspen. "One more story. Come sit with me." She bobbed her head up and down.

"Okay, one more, but then we are all going to bed." Aspen sat next to the little dragon, and she crawled up onto Aspen's lap.

Sid settled down by Aspen and looked at Skye. "Have you told her the story about the three dragon kings yet?"

"No, that's a good one."

Runa watched Skye with wide eyes.

"Once upon a time there was a good king. His followers loved him. Except an evil white dragon from the north. She was powerful and used magic many dragons had forgotten. She became known as the evil white witch. She didn't like the king and wanted to take over, but she was a smart dragon and waited until the king showed weakness."

"What kind of weakness?" Runa asked.

"One that would make it easy for her to become queen of the dragons. She didn't know what kind of weakness she was looking for. She was waiting. You know the gift of the arctic dragons, right?"

"Yeah, they live forever."

Skye laughed. "Not forever, but a lot longer than any of the rest of us. So she grew old in years and strong in her magic and continued to wait. Until one day, she learned a secret about the king. He had a weakness few knew about, and she made plans to kill the king and take over. Quietly, she gathered supporters. Mostly from the arctic dragons but a few from other races too. No one wanted a weak king to reign. She planned her attack, and just before she struck, something extraordinary happened."

"She died!" yelled Runa and laughed at her own joke.

Skye smiled and shook her head. "No, she didn't die. How many dragons are king at once?"

"Only one."

"Exactly. We talked about this earlier today. How does a dragon become king?"

"He turns black."

"That's right. On the eve of the evil witch's attack, two more dragon kings were found."

"How's that possible?"

"No one knows. But the evil dragon knew she could fight a weak king, but she didn't stand a chance against three kings. So she retreated, but instead of giving up, she gathered more supporters and divided the dragons. Soon, instead of a small fight, the dragons were at war. Everyone took a side, and no one knew who would win, the white witch or the three kings.

"But the kings discovered a source of strength the witch didn't have. They found themselves queens that were even more powerful than themselves. Together, the six of them fought the white witch and defeated her and lived happily ever after."

Runa bobbed her head for a second. "Who reigned then? You can't have three kings?"

"Of course you can. They reigned together for a thousand years."

Sid eyebrows creased together, and he frowned. Aspen was curious about what was bothering him but didn't want to ask him about it in front of Skye and Runa.

"Bed, now," said Aspen

Runa looked up at Aspen. "Yes, mother." She flew off down the hall.

"Who are you sleeping with tonight?" Aspen yelled after her.

"Rowan." She turned and glared at Aspen, misjudged her distance, and slammed right into the door. She fell but got right back up. "Where'd that door come from?"

Sid chuckled behind Aspen. "She's a mess. You ready to go to sleep?"

Aspen took his hand. "Sure. You okay? You looked like something was bothering you."

"Yeah. Skye modified the story a little bit. First off, not all the kings survive. In fact only one does." He looked down at her. "Also, it's a prophecy, not a story."

Aspen's stomach clenched. "Sounds scary."

"It's one of those stories we hear and hope never happens." He scratched his head. "I realized something as Skye was telling the story."

"What's that?"

"I'm going to be a weak king."

Aspen grasped his hands. "No, you won't. You'll be a great king."

"No, Aspen, you don't understand. Because I can't take a queen, I literally will be physically weaker than other kings. I've known that since we started all this, but the prophecy worries me."

Aspen leaned up and kissed him lightly on the lips. "I only see one king around here, so I'm guessing the prophecy isn't being fulfilled today. Let's go to bed."

CHAPTER 25

THAT NIGHT SID woke to the door creaking open. He looked up but didn't see anything. There was a little light coming in from the hallway, but Aspen was curled up tight next to him, and he didn't want to leave to go shut the door. He kissed her softly on the forehead and fell back to sleep almost immediately.

What he didn't see was the little dragon who landed softly on his headboard, muttering things under her breath.

"You think I'm too young, huh? You think I can't handle the responsibility? Well, I'll show you. Sure, I haven't reached my hundredth birthday yet, but I can decide who I want to pledge my loyalty to. You dumb oaf."

She leaned over and placed her snout on his forehead. He shifted and brushed his hair. Runa jerked back and nearly fell off the headboard. She righted herself and waited. After he finished moving around, she remembered that she was supposed to say something first. She thought back to what Skye had taught her. Course Skye thought she was just teaching her history, but really Runa just wanted to know how the loyalty seal worked.

"On behalf all the underground dragons, I pledge my loyalty to you."

Then she placed her snout back on his forehead, and she felt her chest burn. She hoped he wouldn't feel it too and wake up. He rolled onto his back, and she took flight. He rubbed at a spot on his chest, a spot that was deep brown and had her name on it. He rolled back over but didn't wake up.

She flew out of the room in search of a mirror, thoroughly pleased with herself.

CHAPTER 26

SID STEPPED OUT of the shower, wrapped a towel around himself, and wiped off the mirror. It was still foggy, so he turned on the fan. He brushed his teeth and reached for his razor. There were some things that were thoroughly irritating about being human. He was glad he was a guy though and not a girl. That required a lot more work.

The mirror cleared, and the seals reflected back at him. All five of them.

Five?

Sid wiped at the mirror again so he could see the dark brown mark just underneath Skye's. The circle centered around Runa's name.

He was going to kill her. Probably right after her father killed him.

He stormed out of the bathroom and hollered. "Runa, get your tiny self up here."

Aspen sat up and sucked in a breath. He looked over at her. A red flushed filled her cheeks. He gave her a crooked grin.

"Like what you see?"

She nodded then looked away. "Why are you yelling for Runa?"

He sat down on the edge of the bed. "She didn't listen." He pointed at his chest.

Aspen shook her head. "That little girl's got a death wish. I'll go find her. You get dressed."

As she stood, she let her fingers trail along his leg, and he nearly forgot that he was pissed as hell at Runa.

Sid waited until Aspen left the room before he went in search of clothes. He couldn't let Runa go home at all. She was stuck with them for a while. He wondered if that was why she did it. Aspen came back a few minutes later with Runa on her shoulder.

Runa jumped off and bowed deeply to Sid.

He rolled his eyes. "What do you think you're doing?"

She peeked up. "Showing my respects, sir."

"Nothing's changed."

"Yes, it has. Now that I've pledged my loyalty to you, you're my king."

Sid grimaced. "That was foolish. You know that if I die, so do you."

She jumped up on the bed. "But I wasn't living any sort of life before I escaped with you. Really, it was Aspen I should've pledged my loyalty to. She's the one who rescued me. But that wouldn't help you. You needed me. It could take you months to find an unmarked underground dragon."

"I don't want you think that I'm ungrateful, but this was rash. This has consequences far beyond anything you can comprehend."

She rose up on her haunches and lifted her neck here. "Listen here..."

A door slammed, and a woman wailed. Sid and Aspen looked at each other for a half second before racing down the stairs. His mother was standing in the entryway, sobbing and carrying on. She shouted incomprehensible things, pulled at her hair, and stomped on the ground.

Aspen took a tentative step forward. "What's wrong with her?"

Sid shook his head. "I have no idea." He moved toward his mother. A wave of grief hit him, and he immediately blocked all her feelings.

"Dead," Athena screamed. "He's dead, and it's all your fault." She fell onto him and beat at his chest with her fists.

CHAPTER 27

ANOTHER DEATH. ASPEN stared at the floor, not wanting to meet anyone's eyes.

"Mom, what happened?" Sid pulled his mother in for a tight hug, and she sobbed into his shoulder.

"Your father is dead."

"How?" He squeezed his eyes shut, but a few tears escaped anyway. Aspen had never lost a parent. She didn't have the foggiest idea how to comfort him.

Athena looked up and wiped at her eyes. "I don't know. I felt our connection sever. He's dead."

Sid's head snapped up. "Go find Pearl, Skye, and Theo. Have them meet me in the front yard."

Aspen raced to the kitchen and found the girls talking.

"What was all that racket?" Pearl asked.

"It's your mom. You need to go now, you too, Skye. Sid said to meet him out front."

Aspen raced upstairs and flung Theo's door open. His room was empty. She took out her phone and called him, but he didn't answer. She called Ella, and she answered on the third ring.

"What's up?"

"Is Theo with you?"

"Nope. I haven't seen him in a few days. He was supposed to come over last night, but he never showed. Everything okay?"

"Not really. Sid needs him. His dad died."

"Oh honey, give him my condolences. If I see Theo, I'll send him your way. If you see him first, tell him I'm pissed that he left me hanging."

"Okay. Thanks, Ella."

Aspen hung up the phone, made her way back downstairs, and found Athena slumped on the floor by the front door, crying. Aspen left her there, went outside, and her mouth dropped open in awe. Eagles filled the entire yard. Sid had transformed into a dragon as well as Skye and Pearl. The sight of the three of them was stunning.

…find him. Search everywhere. It's possible he was out of the park as well. Alert the other animals and send me a message as soon as you find something.

When he stopped speaking, they all took flight. If Aspen wasn't so shocked by the situation, she would've taken a picture. The sight of the hundreds of eagles and the three dragons lifting off of the ground at once was breathtaking. They were gone before she could tell Sid she couldn't find Theo. She went back inside and crouched down next to Athena.

She put her hand on her shoulder. "Come on, let's find somewhere more comfortable to sit."

Athena didn't respond, so Aspen stood up and pulled on her arms. Her legs were shaky, and she trembled with sobs. Aspen led her into the theater room and set her down gently on the couch. She gathered her in her arms. This wasn't Aspen's normal behavior, but she didn't know what else to do. The woman continued to cry.

After about fifteen minutes, her tears started to subside.

"Can I get you anything? Tea? Coffee? Chocolate?"

Athena pulled away and shook her head. Aspen handed her a tissue.

Athena blew her nose and looked at Aspen with red eyes. "Thank you. I didn't know it was possible to feel this awful."

"How do you know he's dead?"

"There's a connection that forms when you are bonded. It's different from when you're sealed. You quite literally become one soul. I felt it cut off. It was like tearing my soul in half. It physically hurt. But it was nothing compared to the pain I felt when I realized what it meant. He's still young. I don't know how I'll live another two hundred years without him. It's awful. I don't want to go on living."

"I know it's hard, but you have to. For your sake, for your kids' sake. Sid needs your support."

She snorted. "Yeah, he'll probably die as well. Then I'll have lost both of my boys. I guess I'll find out what that pain is like too. What am I going to do?"

Aspen's heart stilled. She didn't know how help this woman. "First off, Sid is going to live. I'll see to that. Second, you're going to grieve and probably cry a lot. But you'll live."

They sat in silence for a few moments and Aspen finally stood up. "Would it help if I put a movie on? It will take your mind off things."

Athena nodded.

"Do you have any preferences?"

"They didn't have movies when I did my human experience, but I saw one a few years ago with Pearl. I don't care. Something light."

Aspen headed to the Disney/Pixar section and put on *Toy Story*. Then she went into the kitchen. Rowan had a bag of marshmallows, and Runa was cooking them with her flames. Apparently her fire changed color as well.

Rowan turned around. "You want one?"

"No. Sid's dad died."

Rowan caught the marshmallow that had just been toasted with a brilliant green flame. "Ouch," he said and dropped the marshmallow. He looked at the gooey mess on the floor. "Did you say Sid's dad died?"

"Yeah, and his mom is in the theater room."

"Really? Where's Sid?" Rowan took off his glasses and rubbed at his eyes.

"Out trying to find him."

Runa hopped off the table and flew toward the theater room.

Aspen and Rowan followed her. She settled on the couch next to Athena and laid her head on her lap. Athena put her hand on the small dragon's head. Aspen and Rowan sat on the other side of the couch.

The movie started, but Aspen watched Athena instead of the screen. Her red hair hung in strings around her tear-streaked face.

Aspen had never seen someone who was in so much pain. She hoped she'd never have to feel that kind of sorrow in her life. She knew she wouldn't be able to handle it.

CHAPTER 28

THE THREE DRAGONS spread out. Sid was alone as he flew around south Yellowstone in search of his father's body. His heart hurt, but he also felt a burning anger. He wanted nothing more than to rip whatever dragon did this limb from limb. Sid's father wasn't a warrior. He was a tracker. He wished now he had sent him out with a partner. His dad might be alive now. Shame replaced his anger. He would make a horrible king if these were the kinds of decisions he made.

An eagle flew near him.

He's been spotted, Your Majesty.

Sid jerked around. *Where?*

Near Lamar Valley.

Sid didn't bother answering. He just turned and flew north.

He saw Pearl and Skye first. He landed next to his father's lifeless body. His wings had been ripped to shreds, and there were bite marks everywhere on his scales. It looked like he put up a good fight.

Skye nudged him. *We can't let him just lie there. Let's take care of him and get back to your mother.*

I can't believe he's dead. Sid felt a hole open in his chest. When his mother told him his dad was dead, he didn't want to believe it. But seeing his dead body made it real. His dad always had his back, and now he was gone.

You take his head, and Pearl and I will each take a flank.

Sid watched as Pearl's and Skye's blue and silver flames devoured the body. His father slowly disappeared. Soon it was Sid's turn. He let out a jet of black flames, and his father was gone. Their flames lingered for about thirty seconds, and when done, there was shiny gold gemstone about the size of an ostrich's egg in place of the ashes. Sid picked it up with one of his claws and took off back toward his house.

He would make sure this monster died a slow and painful death.

CHAPTER 29

THE MOVIE WAS almost finished when Aspen heard voices floating down the hall. Athena jumped up and ran for the door. Sid, Skye, and Pearl stood in the entryway. Pearl was crying, and the rest were subdued.

Athena ran up to Sid. "Did you find him?"

Sid held out a large golden crystal. "We did."

Athena gripped it tight, fell to the floor, and buried her face in the stone.

They were all sitting in the kitchen when Theo entered the room.

"Where the hell have you been?" Sid asked.

"What do you mean?"

"I go to DC for a couple of days and come back, and you've gone missing."

Theo puffed out his chest. "I told you I was going to California to visit some of my old friends. If you were going to be gone, there was no reason to hang out here."

"Well, you picked a crappy time to leave."

"What's that supposed to mean?"

"My dad died."

"What?" Theo clenched his fists.

"That's why my mom is here."

Athena got up and gave Theo a massive hug. "I've missed you."

He returned the hug. "I'm so sorry. I had no idea."

"Next time answer your phone."

"Sorry, we spent most of the time out on the water. I left my phone here."

"You should call Ella. She's pretty worried," Aspen said.

"Oh yeah, I forgot to tell her I was going."

Aspen snorted. She knew this behavior. She'd seen her sister do this a thousand times. Theo was trying to break up with Ella, but blowing it big time.

"You know, you can just tell her. She'll understand."

Theo creased his eyebrows.

"You want to break up with Ella. I can tell. There are easier ways to do it than to just up and run away to California for a few days."

"No, that's not it." Theo squeezed his eyes shut for a second.

Aspen started to argue with him, but Sid interrupted, sitting down next to Theo. "Can you replace my dad's mark for me?" He pointed to his missing circle.

Theo didn't say anything, and Sid worried that maybe he would say no.

"He most certainly will not." Athena stood. "You are my son. You will have my mark."

Pearl blanched. "I'd really rather Theo do it. I've already lost my father. If Sid fails, then I'll lose both my mother and my brother as well. That's not fair."

Athena turned to her. "We're all in this together. We keep it in the family. Blood is stronger than friendship. By giving Sid my loyalty, he'll be stronger than if it was Theo. I'm sorry, Pearl, but I won't let any other royal dragon do this."

Sid and Athena left everyone else to go outside and take care of replacing the royal seal. Afterwards, Athena studied all the marks.

"Any plans for the other three?"

"Pearl has contacts out looking for a river dragon. So far nothing. I have a canyon dragon who will do it as soon as everyone else does. I have no idea about the arctic dragon."

Athena paused. "Let me think about that. Most of them are loyal only to Winerva, but I bet we can find someone that wants to see her off the council."

CHAPTER 30

CHRISTMAS MORNING ASPEN woke early and made her way to the kitchen. As she neared the room, she heard shouts. She hurried out to see what was going on. Runa was cowering on the floor, and a bright yellow dragon the size of a golden retriever hovered over her.

"What in the stars are you doing here?" the yellow dragon roared.

"Just playing, mama, I like it here."

"I get home from visiting your aunt, and I find that my daughter has run away. Explain yourself."

"Daddy keeps me cooped up all the time. I just wanted to see the sun. Don't be mad."

The yellow dragon sighed. "I'm not mad. Not really, but I do wish you'd found a way to secure permission. I've never seen your father so angry. You have to come back with me."

Runa stood up, her head reaching the chest of the yellow dragon. "No, mama, I'm not coming home. I want to stay here with Obsidian and Aspen."

She took flight and landed on Aspen's shoulder. She buried her face in Aspen's hair. Aspen grabbed an apple from the bowl on the counter and sat down at the breakfast table.

"So, you're a river dragon. What's your name?"

"I'm Stella, and I want my daughter back."

"I'm not keeping her here."

Runa stuck her head out. "Yes, you are. Tell her I'm not going back with her. I can't anyway. I'm sealed to Sid."

Stella's face turned red, and yellow puffs of smoke came out of her nostrils. "You're just a baby! How can you be sealed to anyone? Who's Sid?"

"Mama, it's not that kind of sealing." Runa stuck out her chest. "He's the king, and I swore allegiance to him."

Stella's face went as pale as the moon. Aspen didn't know that was even possible. She chewed and swallowed a bite of her apple.

"I'm going to go get Sid. He can explain all of this."

He was pulling a hoodie on over his t-shirt. "You're just going to have to take that off again."

Sid gave her a crooked grin. "Merry Christmas to you too."

Aspen laughed. "As much as I'd love to stay in here with you, we can't. There is a furious yellow dragon in the kitchen wondering why on earth her daughter swore allegiance to you."

Aspen watched the color drain from his face. At least the two dragons would match.

Stella studied Sid as he approached.

"I would like to see the marks."

He took off his shirt, and Aspen once again completely enjoyed the view.

"You are missing a river dragon."

"Yes, I have not yet secured their loyalty."

"Then I will give you mine."

Sid opened his mouth. Closed it again and then finally asked, "Why?"

"Because my daughter is already entangled in this. By swearing my loyalty to you, I've gotten you one step closer to surviving, which means she'll survive. I think I can also get you another of your missing marks."

"I appreciate it, but I already have a canyon dragon. He just didn't want to pledge his loyalty until I secured all the others."

"With all due respect, Your Majesty, I have an arctic dragon. Not a canyon dragon."

Sid's eyes bugged, and Aspen's head spun. If that was true, then they had everything they needed. He would survive and be king in spite of the obstacles placed before him.

"I hope you don't mind the rush, but I'd rather like to get this over with."

Sid and Stella entered the cave. Sid had no idea where he was. Somewhere in Canada. It was beautiful, but completely isolated.

"Olwen, it's me, Stella."

There is someone else with you. I can sense him.

"Yes, I've brought someone who wants to help you."

They flew around a bend, and Sid saw one of the largest dragons he'd ever seen. He was the size of a castle in Europe. His ice blue eyes followed Sid and Stella as they landed.

How is this dragon going to help me? He's king. He won't go against his council.

"He's pissed off the council and is trying to create his own."

The dragon brought his house-sized head down and blinked at them. Stella must've looked like a fly to him.

You've invoked the loyalty seals?

I have.

How many do you have left?

Two. Arctic and canyon. I have a canyon dragon who has sworn to pledge his loyalty once I secure the rest.

The dragon lifted his head and moved back several feet.

I have not seen many dragons in the last several years. My race despises me. I will not be welcomed among them.

You will have a home with the royal dragons. I can promise you that. You're welcome to come with us tonight if you wish. Even if you choose not pledge your loyalty to me. No one deserves to be isolated like this. Why are you here anyway?

That I cannot divulge. I discovered things I shouldn't have, and Winerva spread rumors about me. I could not stay home. They would've killed me. Stella is the only dragon who has visited me in the last two hundred years. I would rather wait until you succeed before I come out of hiding. Until then, it will not be safe for me.

Will you pledge to me?

After a very long pause, he brought his head down, and Sid worried that he'd be crushed like a bug, but the dragon rested his snout on Sid's head, and Sid felt his chest burn once again.

Thank you.

Good luck. It will be nice to have company again. Send Stella when it is safe for me to come.

I'll send a few royal dragons with her to escort you to Yellowstone so that you will be safe. I look forward to meeting with you again.

Aspen paced by the door. They'd had too many close calls between Apollo and the eagles, and she worried constantly for Sid's safety.

"Would you sit down?" Athena said.

"Like you're not worried about him out there."

"Of course I am, but you don't see me pacing. You're making me nervous. Sit down."

Aspen crossed her arms and stared at Athena. "I should've gone with him."

Athena snorted. "You think you are always going to go with him? If you were his queen, you'd be able to, but you won't be his queen. You're going to have to stay home most of the time. Get used to waiting. I can't believe he went and sealed himself to you."

Aspen rolled her eyes. Athena said something similar every time they were together and Sid wasn't around.

"Skye, do you want help?" Aspen asked. She was making a cake or something. Aspen never bothered to even ask what it was anymore since Skye always had something in the mixer.

She shook her head. "I've got it, thanks."

The front door slammed, and both Aspen and Athena ran to the foyer. Sid grinned from ear to ear.

"Got it," he said and whipped his shirt off. Underneath Runa's mark was a bright white one. Aspen flung herself at him. He lifted her up in his embrace and whispered in her ear. "We won. I can't believe we won."

"I can. Your Majesty." She pulled away, and he gave her a serious look. "What?" she asked.

"It sounds weird coming from you. Almost makes it real."

"No more seriousness tonight. Let's celebrate."

"Sure. But first I need to send an eagle to get Helios."

Sid went outside, and everyone else gathered in the kitchen. They laughed and talked until late in the night.

When they climbed into bed, Sid grabbed Aspen's ankle and traced her tattoo.

"It's weird to think this all started with this little mark."

Aspen grinned. "I know. What do the words mean? You never told me."

He traced at the words and muttered, "Nin Meleth, Nin Aran." He looked up at her. "It means my love, my king."

Aspen slipped her foot out of his grip and grabbed his. "What does yours mean? It's different. Nin Meleth, Nin Bereth."

"It means my love, my queen."

"But I could never be your queen. I'm not a dragon."

He pulled her close to him. "That's not exactly true."

She laughed. "I'd know it if I were a dragon. Wouldn't I?"

He grinned. "You're not a dragon. But the dragon queen is always human."

"What?" She pulled away from him.

"Yeah, it's how we maintain our human forms. The last queen was Olivia. She died a few years before the king did."

"You mean we could've fixed this all by just asking the council to make me your queen?"

He shook his head. "You'll never be my queen. I won't let you do that."

"Why not?" Aspen pulse raced, and her face flushed. The solution was right in front of them, and no one said a word to her.

"Because most potential queens don't survive the testing. I'm not going to risk your life."

"You were willing to die, but you weren't willing to let me try? How is that fair?" She scrambled out of bed. "I can't believe you lied to me."

"I didn't lie to you. I just didn't tell you everything. It doesn't matter now. I'll be king, and you will be with me."

"But I won't really. I'll just be some girl who's hanging around. This isn't right."

He shook his head. "Even Olivia was a little mentally unstable because of her testing, and she survived. I won't put you through that. Can you come back to bed? We need to rest. Tomorrow will be a happy day, but long."

Aspen climbed back under the covers, but was still furious. This wasn't over. Not by a long shot.

She lay awake for a long time, fuming. Sid snored lightly next to her. How the hell could he sleep at a time like this? It felt like she'd just drifted off when she felt Sid thrashing. Her eyes flashed open as two men dragged him out of bed.

"Hey," she yelled and ran for them. One took a cloth out of his pocket and put it over Sid's mouth and nose. Sid went limp in their arms. Aspen flung herself at the other man, hitting and kicking. He took a swing backwards and nailed her right in the head. She fell, and everything went black.

Aspen wasn't sure how long she was out, but her head was killing her. She could barely stand. Sid was gone. She squeezed her eyes shut and opened them again, trying to remember what happened. Then an image flashed in her head of Sid being dragged away. Panic bloomed in her chest as she stumbled down the stairs into the kitchen.

"Someone took Sid," Aspen said to Pearl and Skye, and collapsed into a chair, holding her head.

Both women jerked their heads to her. "What?"

"They knocked me out. I don't know who it was. Two men. Super strong."

An eagle pecked at the window, and Pearl spun around. She opened the window and the eagle flew in. Pearl stared at the eagle for a few seconds. Then she sank into her chair.

"I've been summoned to a council meeting. They're holding a trial for treason."

Aspen creased her eyebrows. "Treason?"

"Obsidian," Pearl said.

Aspen stood up. "I'm coming with you."

Pearl laughed. "Oh no you won't. If I show up with you, Sid will kill me right after the council kills you." She put her hand on Aspen's. "Listen, I'll do whatever I can for him, but this doesn't look good at all. He sealed himself to a human girl and tried to form his own council. They won't let him live. Prepare yourself for that reality."

CHAPTER 31

PEARL SWEPT FROM the room, and Skye put her arm around Aspen. "Are you okay?"

"No. I can't think straight. My head is killing me."

"I'll get you some Tylenol. Wait here."

Aspen closed her eyes, and when she opened them again, a huge orange dragon sat on the other side of the window. Skye came back with the Tylenol and squeaked.

Aspen took the medicine from Skye and swallowed it dry. She headed out the side door with Skye on her heels.

Where is Obsidian? the orange dragon asked, his scales glittering in the sunset. His color blended together like a sunset.

"You're too late. He's been taken by the council," Skye said.

Aspen spun around. "Wait, you mean he was the one who was going to pledge his loyalty to Sid?"

Skye nodded.

"Sid told me that if he had a mark from all the races, he would be untouchable. Is that true?"

"Yeah, but it's too late now."

Aspen stared at Skye, baffled at the fact that she hadn't thought of the possibilities yet. The idea that if Sid could be marked by a canyon dragon, then he wouldn't die.

"We need to get to Sid."

Skye snorted. "I'd like to die with some dignity, thank you very much. Not at the hand of some murderous council member."

Aspen rolled her eyes. "You're not going to die. All we need to do is get close enough for Helios to mark Sid, then they can't do anything to him. Right?"

Skye nodded and let out a breath.

"Would you be willing to take that chance?" Skye asked.

Yes. I've thought a lot about what Obsidian said to me when he visited. I was cowardly for not pledging my loyalty then. If I had, he wouldn't be sitting in front of the council right now. It's the least I can do.

"Okay, let's go," Skye said. "I'll take you, because I doubt Helios could find it, but I'm not going to stay. There is still a strong possibility that Sid will die, and I would like to see my parents one more time."

"Wait," shouted a voice from the bushes. "I'm going with." Runa hopped out and looked up at all of them.

"No, you're not. You stay here with Rowan."

"You can't make me stay. I'll just follow."

"She's got a point," said Skye.

Aspen didn't want to waste any more time. If Sid died, Runa would anyway.

"If you can keep up, you can come. Let's go."

CHAPTER 32

S ID WOKE UP in the middle of the council chambers. He'd been here many times before, but never like this. He transformed into a dragon and looked around. Eight dragons surrounded him. It was completely silent. He knew them all and even considered some of them his friends. Hell, Pearl was his sister.

But today, they were his enemies. They were going to kill him.

Xanthous, the river dragon and speaker for the council, spoke out loud.

"We are saddened by this meeting. We expected a lot of things from you, Obsidian. Treason was not one of them."

There was no other way.

"Of course there was. You didn't give us a chance. You just went behind our back and tried to create your own council."

You would've killed me anyway when you found out I sealed myself to Aspen.

The dragon sat back on his haunches. "Maybe. You're sister has told us all, but I'd love to hear the story from your own mouth."

It doesn't matter now. I'd rather get this over with.

Xanthous laughed. "I wish it were that simple, Obsidian, but believe it or not, we haven't decided your fate just yet."

Obsidian froze. *What are you talking about? I sealed myself to a girl who could never be a queen, and I went against the council and formed my own. You said yourself that it was treason.*

"I wish you were our only problem. As bad as it was that you tried to usurp our power, we are more concerned with the other dragon king possibilities. No one knows how they are chosen, and there is one among you who has betrayed us worse than you have."

I don't understand.

"Kingston has sealed himself to an arctic dragon. If you die and he becomes king, we lose the ability to continue to take human form, and we need that to maintain peace with them."

So just kill him too. You don't seem to have a problem with taking out those that oppose you.

"We don't want to be murderers. If you cooperate, we may not need to kill anyone."

Obsidian flicked his eyes to Pearl. *What's he talking about?*

I can't tell you that. I'm sorry. I'm not allowed to divulge information we discuss. Only Xanthous can do that.

"We need the girl," Xanthous said.

Excuse me? What girl?

"The one you sealed yourself to. Aspen."

No way, you leave her out of this.

Xanthous paused for a minute and then smiled at Obsidian. "How fortunate for us. Here she comes."

Obsidian felt a cloud come over his mind. He tried to project a thought out to Xanthous, but he couldn't.

"I'm sorry. We'll remove the block after we've had time to speak with her."

Skye flew south into the park, Runa next to her, her little wings beating four times as often as Skye's. She gained altitude, and Aspen noticed they were flying near Eagle's Peak. Skye crossed over the mountain and circled back to a cave on the other side. She flew straight through the opening. They were in a large tunnel studded with ruby gemstones.

After several feet, she touched down, and Helios landed next to her.

This is where I leave you. I don't expect we'll see each other again. If you survive, tell Rowan that I cared for him a great deal.

"Don't be like that. We're all going to survive."

You have a great deal of courage and faith. I hope you're right.

Skye nudged Aspen with her great head and then flew back out of the cave.

Come on, girl, let's go save Obsidian.

Aspen crawled onto Helios's back, and he flew down the rest of the ruby-studded tunnel and into a huge crater. At the bottom sat Obsidian, surrounded by several dragons of varying color and size. Helios touched down behind him. Aspen scrambled off his back, and immediately several gold and silver dragons surrounded them. They descended on Helios and wouldn't let him pass, separating them from Obsidian and the council. Fear. A word that had no place in Aspen's vocabulary. It crept up on her when she least expected it, and now she found herself afraid. If Helios couldn't get to Obsidian, they would all die.

Runa nudged Aspen's knee and took flight. "Grab my feet."

Aspen didn't hesitate. She held tight to Runa's feet and was lifted out of the middle of the circle of dragons that surrounded them. To her surprise, none of the gold and silver dragons tried to stop them, instead they moved in tighter around Helios.

Runa set her down next to Obsidian, then landed and kept her body close to Aspen.

Aspen knew that her life was about to end, but her fear ran deeper for the dragons sitting next to her, who would also be killed. Because of her. Never before had her dangerous adventures threatened others.

She put her hand on Obsidian's side and felt the fire within. His heart raced.

Obsidian talk to me.

A voice answered, but it was not Obsidian. *He can't talk to you, foolish girl. We've forbidden it.*

Aspen smiled because six weeks ago, had she found herself surrounded by eight dragons, she would've been ecstatic and enamored. It said a lot for Obsidian to hold such sway over her that she'd hardly noticed them.

The circular cavern was wide and deep. Nine pots encircled the room, all lit by different colored flames. All except one, which sat at the front of the room, unlit and alone.

In front of each flame sat a dragon of the same color. Bright blue and orange. Brilliant red and lemon yellow. Violet and green, silver, brown, and snow white. They varied in size as well. Of course the smallest was the tiny underground dragon. The white dragon was taller than Aspen's house.

The little yellow dragon cocked his head at Aspen, and then he spoke. "You must be Aspen. We were just talking about you."

"Yes," she replied.

"You'll have to forgive Obsidian's rudeness at the moment. We have forbidden him to speak. Although, I'm sure if he could, he would have a lot to say. He was adamantly against going to get you. How fortunate we are that you came to us. You couldn't have known, of course, why we were coming for you. Why are you here?" His voice squeaked.

"I've come to ask you not to kill Obsidian." Aspen knew what they were going to say, and she prepared herself to argue, and tried to muster up her courage to make another bold request.

The dragons shifted around her, probably talking to one another. Their heads would lean this way and that. Every once in a while, a puff of colored smoke would escape from their nostrils. After what seemed like an hour, but was more like ten minutes, the yellow dragon spoke again.

"Do you understand the magnitude of Obsidian's crimes?"

"You mean falling in love with me or trying to save his own life, because I see no crime in those things."

The little dragon crawled closer to her. "You are brave, aren't you? Yes, you are right. He has put us in a very difficult situation. On the one hand, he has created a situation where he cannot have a queen. He also tried to displace us as a council by creating his own."

"Why can he not have a queen?"

"Because he's sealed himself to you, my dear."

Aspen tried to stand a little taller as she made her next request. "So make me the dragon queen. I know she has to be human."

Aspen felt Obsidian shake next to her. The air in the pit was suddenly warmer. Wings opened and closed. Feet stomped on the floor.

"That is a very bold request, Aspen. But we dismissed you as a possible candidate weeks ago. Pearl presented your name to the council when Obsidian first developed feelings for you."

Aspen crossed her arms. "Why was I dismissed?" Her pulse quickened, and she narrowed her eyes at them.

"You are too young for one thing. Add to that, as we searched your ancestry, we found no leadership in your bloodline, and the women in your family have weak seed."

"Excuse me. My mother had three children."

"With a lot of help. She had several miscarriages, and with both of her successful pregnancies she was on bed rest for most of it."

Aspen had no idea. How the hell did they know all this? She'd have to ask her mother about that when they got out of this mess.

"I don't see what my family history has to do with my ability to be a good candidate. I want this. I want to be your queen."

"Do you realize what being a queen entails?"

"No, but I'm sure I can handle it."

"You must embrace our race. It is possible you will never speak to another human again. Are you willing to give that up?"

Aspen thought for a second. No more contact with her parents, Rowan, or Ella. Obsidian would be her sole companion. Well, him and all the rest of the dragons. Could she give up her human life for him? Did she even have a choice?

"Of course."

"You will act as our mother. You must love us as you would your own children, your own family. We all know you love and care for Obsidian, but can you love the rest of us? We who are despised by humankind, considered monsters."

"I've loved the dragons for a long time. Long before I met Obsidian. That will not be a problem."

The yellow dragon looked at Pearl and nothing was said for several moments. Then he turned back to face her. "Pearl has confirmed what you have said is true, how intriguing. But being the queen can also be tedious and at times dangerous. Can you do that? Are you willing to be put to the test?"

Aspen didn't hesitate. "Yes."

Obsidian whimpered. Aspen placed her hand on his side, and he shivered. Aspen wished he could speak to her.

"Fine then, we shall put you to the test. If you pass, you become queen. If you don't, you die along with Obsidian as well as all the dragons who pledged their loyalty to him. Pearl, please take Obsidian to the observation area. Anasazi, please fetch Everett. We shall begin as soon as he joins us."

CHAPTER 33

HELIOS IS DEAD. I am personally going to rip his wings off. Why did he bring Aspen with him? Sid asked.

Now you calm down, Pearl replied. *I'm sure he had his reasons.*

Runa bobbed up and down next to him. "She wasn't about to be left behind. I can understand that. I wouldn't either."

They landed on the edge of a cliff high above the pit. They had a good view of the entire cavern. Aspen sat in the middle of the circle of council dragons. No human her age had ever been placed in front of the council before, and most women had three to four years of training prior to the test. This was foolish, and she was about to die. He could not save her. By interfering with the test, he condemned himself to death.

What is going to happen? Sid asked. He was not alive when the prior queen had been chosen. He had never witnessed the test. As king, it was his duty to watch his future queen prove herself. He did not wish to watch her die.

Your guess is as good as mine, little brother. Before Aunty Ashe died, she tutored me in how to administer my portion of the test. She had witnessed two queens pass. She also watched eight women fail. Most of the council is new to the test. Of course Winerva has seen them all, and Kairi *was on the council when the last queen was chosen.*

Could Aspen die during your part?

No, but she might go insane. It is beginning. I must go take my place on the council. Everett will stay here with you and explain what is going on. Whatever happens, do not interrupt. It is our duty to ensure that she is a proper queen. Runa, you stay put as well.

The old golden dragon flopped down next to Sid. When the original truce between the humans and dragons had been formed, Everett had been there as a young dragon. He was graced with longevity from the leader of the arctic clan. He had been around ever since to oversee the test and perform the king's bond and only came out during the ceremonies. No one knew his true age or the details concerning the prophecy of his future death.

I understand that she came forward and demanded to be the dragon queen, Everett said.

Something like that. She is very headstrong. I've never met anyone, dragon or human, who is as tenacious as she is. Sid watched as the eight dragons circled her. She stood in the middle, unmoving. Sid didn't even think she was shaking.

You are feeling a great deal of fear, why?

She is very young and has not been trained in any way. I fear for her life.

Women die during the test all the time. The weak do not survive. No king has ever feared for the life of a woman before.

Aspen and I know each other quite well. I am very fond of her.

Ah, you are in love before the test. This has never happened. I shall have to take great care in explaining to you what is going on. He scooted forward and hung his withered snout over the edge of the pit to better observe the proceedings. *You might as well relax. We will be here for a while.*

Sid settled down and stuck his head out over the edge. As much as he didn't want to see, he had to in case he needed to intervene. The old dragon beside him continued to prattle on.

Each member of the council will test her in the extremes of their own gifts. Often they are not present at the actual test. For example, once your sister allows Aspen to use the gift of feeling, she will leave and join us up here. Pearl will not be able to bear being in the same room as the test. The pain will be too great. Aspen herself will not know what her test is. She may not even understand that she is able to feel what others are feeling until it is too late.

Sid grew frustrated with the lack of motion in the pit. *Is there any way we can listen to the conversation?* He interrupted.

No, not unless you are canyon. You know that.

Sequoia, the squat woodland dragon, stepped forward. Aspen turned and closed her eyes. A door on the far wall opened, and in walked Damien. Sid cringed. He hadn't been expecting Damien to show up. The council would know Aspen had seen him before too. Damn canyon dragon. If not for him, Aspen and Damien could both act like they'd never met before. Sid watched him slowly make his way across the floor. The scars across his belly still oozed with pus and blood.

Aspen's task is to show compassion for the disfigured dragon, Everett said. *I don't think I've ever seen one as ugly as him. This task always amuses me. It is generally first and should be the easiest, and yet every woman struggles with this one. Some women scream when they open their eyes. Others cringe and back away. Technically to pass the task they are supposed to engage the dragon in a conversation, but only a few dragon queens actually do that. Most pass simply by enduring a half hour in his presence. Damien is new. The disfigured dragon before him passed away a few years ago.*

Aspen opened her eyes and smiled at Damien. Of course, she didn't scream or even cringe.

She waved his head down, and he lowered it so he was eye level with her. She took his broken snout into her hands and kissed the top of his nose. Sid heard a collective gasp from the council. He looked over and saw Everett grinning.

She's got courage, doesn't she? he asked.

Yeah, too much, Sid replied.

CHAPTER 34

"DAMIEN, IT IS good to see you again," Aspen said, looking up at the pitiful dragon.

That it is.

"So, uh, this is a test. What am I supposed to do?"

Damien's whole body shook like Sid's did when he laughed in dragon form.

Your task is to show compassion to me, by conversing with me and not fearing my appearance. Since we've already met, I'm not sure what you are supposed to do.

Aspen supposed that most women, when faced with Damien, would be scared. She would have to think of a different way to show compassion than to just have a conversation with him. She spun around, seeking the council member who had the same red scales as Damien, and stood in front of him.

"What's your name?"

I am Eros.

"Eros, right. Do you have the power to allow Damien to see his son?"

Of course, but I will not grant it. Those were the terms of his punishment. He was able to live, but he cannot see his son.

"How many years has it been?"

I'm not clear on the timing.

Four hundred and thirty-three years, interrupted Damien.

"Four hundred and thirty-three years is a very long time. Do you not think he has suffered enough? He is repentant. He is sad. Allow him this mercy."

Beg all you want, little girl. It is not your decision to make.

She backed up for a moment and thought about what he said. If she made it out of this alive, she'd be queen. She staggered a little at the idea. Up until this moment, she'd only thought of saving her life and Sid's. But now, she realized this had much bigger implications.

She faced the whole council.

"My first act as queen will be to allow Damien to return to his homeland and be reunited with his son. If he is unable to make the journey due to his injuries, then we will send royal ambassadors to bring his son here. This is not a request or a suggestion, but a demand."

None of the council members moved. Sid wasn't sure if that was because they were talking to her or because they were all still stunned by Aspen's behavior. No one had ever shown Damien such respect and attention or treated the council with less respect.

Sequoia returned to her place in the circle.

Eros, the blazing fire dragon, took his place in front of Aspen.

The enchantments begin, Everett said.

What do you mean? Sid asked.

The purpose of the fire dragon's test is to see if she can withstand temptation and not give in to her passion.

How do they do that?

They put her in an enchanted place with a male dragon in his human form. He attempts to seduce her. The council will always choose a dragon that is adept at seducing young human women. Once the enchantment is in place, she will no longer be aware of the council's presence. We will be able to see all that happens, but we will not be able to hear anything.

Sid stared at him horrified. He was supposed to watch while another seduced Aspen? *Uh, do most women pass this test?* Sid asked.

The fire dragons don't care if she passes or not. They just like seducing people. She will move on from the test no matter what. You should be relieved. There is nothing to fear from this one.

I have seen only one woman pass not fall for the seducer. She fainted during the first task and did not wake up until the fifth. The poor dragon sent in to seduce her didn't know what to do. She died during the canyon's task.

Why did the test continue even though she was unconscious?

Why not? If she could survive them unconscious, then she could surely survive them awake.

It didn't make sense to Sid, but he wasn't about to argue with the wisest dragon alive. He wondered who they would use for Aspen's test. Since only royal dragons take human forms, it would be someone he knew.

Everett spoke again, *Here he comes.*

The enchanted room was a garden with a waterfall and pond. Aspen sat on a stone bench, her long hair flowing down her back. Sid yearned to be in that garden with her.

Theo approached Aspen, and Sid relaxed. Then he tensed up again. He had to watch Theo seduce his girl. He almost wished it was someone he didn't know very well. After he killed Skye for bringing Aspen, he would cheerfully tear Theo's tail off.

Jealous? Everett inquired.

Sid snarled at him. *Who is being tested here? Me or Aspen?*

Theo sat down on the bench next to Aspen. She smiled at him.

Sid growled.

Everett laughed.

CHAPTER 35

HAD SHE DIED? Was this Heaven? The intoxicating smell of lilies floated by. Birds sang in the trees. A man sat next to her. He looked familiar, but Aspen couldn't place him.

"Who are you?" she asked.

He took her hand in his, and Aspen's heart fluttered. "Who do you think I am?"

"I don't know. Am I dead?"

He grinned at her, and butterflies floated in her stomach. "If you are dead, then I must be an angel. That will work, hmm."

Where was this? She felt no sense of self or identity and couldn't even remember her own name. She felt light and happy and wanted the man sitting next to her. If this was Heaven, she was pleased.

The man stood up and walked away. She didn't want him to leave. She followed. He paused at a patch of flowers and plucked out a lily and slid it into her hair. He moved his hand so that it caressed the curve of her jaw, and his fingers rested lightly on her chin. Her heart raced, and her stomach burned with desire.

"A flower for my angel, for if I'm to be an angel, then so will you."

Aspen watched his mouth as he spoke. He had entrancing lips. She reached her hand up and traced his lips with her fingers. He closed his eyes and sighed. She took advantage of his sightlessness and moved closer to him. When he opened his eyes, he snaked his arms around her waist and pulled tight, his lips on her ear.

"I thought the goal was to make you want me, my dear Aspen, not the other way around."

His words surprised her. Her name. Her name was Aspen. She lived in Yellowstone with a twin brother and her parents. She knew this man. But she couldn't remember who he was.

He pulled away and intertwined his fingers with her, and her mind clouded once again. He led her along a path. The trees over hanged, and the wisteria tickled her nose. He glanced back at her every few seconds and smiled, her stomach flip-flopping each time. She heard the rushing of water.

The path opened to a large pond with a tall waterfall. She knelt down next to the pond and dipped her fingers in it. It was warm, like a bath. The scent of jasmine in the steam. She inhaled. Her angel sat down next her, his back to the pond. He nuzzled her neck, and the butterflies in her stomach fought to get out.

"Would you like to go for a swim?" he asked.

She wished she understood his pull, his magnetism. She'd say yes to just about anything he asked at this point.

"Of course, but I don't have a suit."

"No need for that."

He stood up and began taking off his clothes. Aspen wondered how far this would go. She didn't think sex was allowed in Heaven. She was relieved, yet disappointed, when he stopped at his boxers. He jumped in the water, and she stripped down and followed.

She dove in deep. When she surfaced, he was inches from her. His hands found her ribcage, and his legs teased her. She felt his breath on her ear once again. "Obsidian was a fool for letting you go."

Obsidian. Sid. Her boyfriend.

The angel looked at her again, his face moving toward hers.

The angel had a name. It was Theo. He was dating Ella, and he was about to kiss her.

His lips brushed hers, and she remembered it all. This was a test. A test she was failing. She pulled away, whipped her hand back, and punched Theo as hard as she could and then swam for the shore. She didn't bother picking up her clothes. She ran. There had to be a way out of there. The forest disappeared, and she was in the cave once again.

Aspen appeared surprised to find herself in the pit. Theo sat about ten feet behind her, sopping wet with blood gushing from his nose. Eros scowled at her.

Everett roared with laughter. *I haven't had this much fun in 2000 years. I hope she makes it. She'll be a fabulous queen.*

Fine then, Sid said. *Stop the test right now and declare her queen.*

Everett suddenly calmed. *That is not in my power. She seems strong. She could still survive this.*

Sid was very pleased that she rebuffed Theo. He was still going to punish Theo. He changed back into his dragon form, and Aspen put her clothes back on.

Eros backed up and nodded to Sid's sister. Pearl stepped forward, placed her snout on the top of Aspen's head, and left the room. Aspen turned in a full circle. She rubbed her forehead, then sat on the stone floor and waited.

Your sister just transferred the power to feel what others are feeling to Aspen. Pearl is on her way up here now, Everett said.

Hey, bro, Pearl said. *Damien's in love with your girl. Looks like you'll have some competition after you get out of here.* Theo followed close behind her. Sid glowered at him.

If we get out of here, Sid replied.

Don't be so gloomy, Pearl said. *She is doing unusually well. By the way, we are skipping Xanthous. He said that she passed his test when she demanded to be made the dragon queen.*

What was Xanthous's test?

I'm not exactly sure, since I haven't witnessed it before, but it has something to do with being persuasive. Xanthous is convinced that she can persuade quite well. Oh look, here they come. Each of those five dragons has lost a mate within the last two weeks. They are grieving deeply. We will still feel some of their grief up here, but it will not be unbearable.

Pearl settled next to Everett, and Theo came around to his other side.

You are not welcome to stay and watch the rest.

Oh come on, don't be like that. It's not like I asked to be part of this. The council approached me. No one says no to the council unless they want to die a slow and painful death.

You'll still die a slow and painful death, Sid replied.

Theo sat down next to Sid anyway.

The five dragons circled Aspen and squatted. All of them lowered their heads to the ground as if they were bowing to her. At first, Aspen did not respond at all, she merely stared at them. Then she gripped her head and fell to the ground. Sid jerked, and Pearl wrapped her tail around him.

Aspen wailed. The sound pierced the air and crushed his heart.

Sid tried to move again, but the spikes on Pearl's tail dug into his belly.

Aspen wanted to die. Her body racked with sobs. She felt nothing but sorrow and pain. She struggled to stand, to make sense of this horrid experience. She managed to get to her knees and look around. Though blurry, there were five dragons surrounding her. Two blue ones, a silver, a purple and green, and a red. Sorrow overtook her again, and she collapsed on the floor. It would be better to just give into the darkness, perhaps then there would be no more pain. *Shut up*, she told the voice in her head.

There had to be a purpose, a reason for this pain. The dragons surrounding her had something to do with this. She rolled over and got up on all fours and crawled over to the first dragon. The magnificent blue clouded by her tears. She reached her arms up and hugged the dragon's neck. Aspen felt wings encircle her, and her pain lessened.

The dragon didn't say anything, and neither did Aspen, and her legs still wouldn't work. She crawled over to the other blue dragon and repeated the process. Aspen had calmed down enough to walk now. The silver dragon was thrashing. Getting close without getting hurt would be difficult. After waiting for the dragon to calm, she rushed forward and briefly registered the wing before being tossed into the air. She landed on her back, her head cracking on the floor. Aspen sat up, her ears ringing, physical pain finally greater than the sorrow.

The silver dragon was still in agony. With her eyes squeezed shut, she swung her great head from side to side. Every once in a while, her wings shot out. Aspen waited until she saw an opening again and ran toward her. She latched onto her neck and felt her body shudder. Then the dragon calmed, and her body collapsed on the floor. Aspen let go and moved on to the purple dragon and then the red.

After finishing, she sat down in the middle of them again. Her body was no longer heaving, though tears still flowed down her cheeks. For the first time in her life, she felt that she had a purpose, a reason to be there. She felt more at home with the dragons than she'd ever felt among her friends and family.

Multiple voices assaulted her at once

We were together six hundred and eighty years.

I miss him so much.

I was supposed to die first.

I thought being bonded meant we'd be together forever. Why are we separated now?

I want to join him; I want to die.

Each voice was unique although she had no idea whom each one belonged to. She sent an *I'm so sorry* to each of them. They had each lost someone close, their companion, she guessed. She had never felt grief so deep, not even when Mrs. Dufour died. She wondered if this was what it would be like when Sid died, or would she go first? Either way, she knew now that she would be okay, even if he did die. It wouldn't be pleasant, but she'd survive her grief.

Each dragon thanked her on her way out and asked that Aspen visit in the future. She hoped that meant they thought she'd make it.

Sid was so enraptured by the scene that he did not notice Pearl had let go of him.

I have to go back down, she said, looking concerned.

What's the matter? Sid asked.

She shows a great capacity for compassion, Pearl explained. *She's never going to pass Winerva's test. I'll see you when this is over. Theo, make sure you hang on to Obsidian. He almost flew straight into the middle of the grievers. He would have gone mad before he got there.*

Can do. Have fun down there, Theo said.

Runa, I need you to come with me. Pearl sat back on her haunches.

"Why?" Runa asked.

Because Nedra asked for you. I think he wants your help with his test.

Everett, what is Winerva's test? Sid turned and looked at him.

Let's not get ahead of ourselves. Winerva will be last. I'll tell you then.

How did Aspen not go mad when we would have?

She's human. It's different for them. But not all humans could handle it. She's stronger than you think.

Aspen's head really hurt, but so far she felt like she was doing fairly well. The tiny underground dragon stepped forward.

The underground dragons possess a strength beyond any dragon alive, but we have a disability that prevents us from exercising that strength on a regular basis. Let's see what you can do.

Everything went dark. Aspen wasn't sure what she was supposed to do, but she'd gone blind.

"Help," a voice called, and Aspen's stomach dropped. That was Runa's voice. She ran toward the sound. After a few feet she tripped and fell. Crap.

"Help," Runa called again. "Aspen, hurry."

Aspen took her time, knowing if she rushed, she'd be flat on her face again. The ground underneath her feet was not flat. She stumbled a little, but did not fall. She was getting closer. Runa continued to yell for help.

She shuffled forward, and her right foot didn't connect with the ground. She backed up and got down on her hands and knees. Runa was close. She reached her hand out and found nothing but air. Runa was in a pit. But how deep?

"Runa, are you in the pit?"

"Yeah."

"How far down? Can I jump?"

"I'm on a ledge. Can't see the bottom."

Dammit. Aspen was going to have to climb for her. Luckily, she had a lot of experience. But she'd never done it blind, nor did she climb without proper equipment.

"I need you to tell me when I'm directly above you so that I don't have to climb sideways."

"I can't see you."

"Look up. Can you see my hand?"

Aspen waved her hand over the pit. At least she hoped that was what she was doing. It was hard to tell without her sight.

"Oh, yeah, I see it. Move twenty feet to the left."

Aspen crawled several feet and waved her hand again.

"Closer. Maybe three feet or so. Hurry. This ledge isn't stable."

Aspen snorted. "Why don't you just fly away?"

"Can't. They tied up my wings."

Aspen's stomach clenched. They wouldn't let Runa die. Would they?

"Hang on. I'm coming."

Aspen swung her legs over and tried to find a foothold, but there was nothing. She wiggled a little to the right—the rock face was smooth as glass. She had moved a full ten feet before she found a good foothold. That meant she'd have to climb sideways.

"You need to guide me. How are you doing?"

"Rocks keep falling. Aspen, hurry."

Aspen found another place for her left foot and held on to the top of the ledge as she felt around with for another spot. She found one and scaled down the face of the cliff. Once she got a feel for it, it was easy. Runa shouted directions to her, and she moved quickly. She got stuck when she was directly above Runa and couldn't find anything to hang onto.

"You could jump," Runa said.

Aspen palms began to sweat. Not a good combination with slick rocks. Sid told her that people died during this test. She'd never felt more unsafe in her life.

"You said the ledge wasn't stable."

"I know, but I don't know how else you are going to get down here. There's nothing to hang onto."

"Okay, I'm going to slide to you. Are you sure you're directly beneath me?"

"Yep."

"As soon as I reach you, you need to climb on my back. If that ledge gives way, I'm going to need to find a way to hang on to the cliff. I won't be able to hold onto you too."

"Okay. Hurry."

Aspen closed her eyes for a second. Took a deep breath and fell. She hit the ledge, and immediately it gave way.

"Runa, quick."

Runa climbed on to her back, and Aspen tried to grab ahold of anything that might be sticking out of the cliff face, but they were falling too fast. All she was doing was scraping up her hands.

"Aspen, grab my leg."

Aspen didn't hesitate even though she knew it was suicide. They were falling to their deaths. But she trusted Runa. She grabbed her leg, and soon they were going up instead of down.

"I thought you said you wings were tied up."

"I'm a pretty good actor, huh? I had you going."

"That's not funny."

"I know. But you passed. Thanks for rescuing me."

Runa dumped her on solid ground again, and Aspen's sight came back suddenly.

Very good, Aspen. Good luck with the rest of the test.

Aspen only survived that one because she had extensive knowledge of how to climb. She stood up and waited, positive that this time she'd be stumped.

A bright blue dragon with ice blue eyes stared down at her and a foreboding entered Aspen's heart. This dragon did not have good things in mind for her.

Kairi, the sea dragon stepped forward.

Theo, Everett said. *You might want to hang on to Obsidian.*

Sid froze. This meant something awful was coming. *Everett, you need to tell me what is about to happen.*

If I explain, it will only make it worse. You do know what the sea dragon's gift is, right?

Yes, you can tell them anything, and they will never reveal your secrets.

Correct.

Are they going to try to get Aspen to reveal a secret?

Something like that. Watch.

Theo's tail squeezed Sid. Sid watched as two humans, dragons presumably, entered the cavern. One pushed a long table with straps. The second rolled in a table with several pitchers of water on it.

They approached Aspen and spoke to her.

"Kairi just told you a secret," the first man said. "What did she tell you about this secret?" Sid liked it when they spoke out loud. Then at least he knew what was going on.

"That I am not to reveal it to anyone, even in the face of death," Aspen said.

"And did you agree?"

"Yes, of course. I keep my word and my secrets."

"We'll see about that, please lay down on the table," said the second man.

Aspen did as she was told. The men bound both her arms and legs. They tilted the table slightly so that her feet were elevated and placed a cloth over her mouth and nose. The first man held her head in place, and the second took a pitcher of water and poured it onto the cloth.

At first, Aspen did not react, and then she strained against her bonds. Her whole body flailed. Sid did not understand what was happening.

After about thirty seconds, they put the pitcher down and removed the cloth. Aspen gasped for air.

"Will you tell me the secret now?"

"No," she rasped and then coughed violently.

In spite of her coughing he replaced the cloth and poured the water again. Both her nose and mouth were covered.

Everett, what are they doing to her?

He sighed. *They are filling her lungs with water.*

You mean they are drowning her?

Some drown, yes. It is really more the feeling of drowning. I'm told it's dreadful. Kairi and her ancestors have been doing the same test for thousands of years. The first woman I watched blurted the secret right after the first pitcher. The second died. I believe it was the fifth woman that actually survived. If they tell the secret, they are killed instantly. Out of all the women who last this long, I'd say a third make it through. They will stop when she loses consciousness. The women who survive pass out after the third or fourth pitcher.

The man in the pit removed the cloth a second time, and Aspen spat in his face. He laughed as he replaced the cloth. Again her body squirmed and fought against the bonds. Again she did not reveal the secret. Sid willed her to pass out. He couldn't stand to see her in such agony. After the fifth pitcher, she vomited. They allowed her to turn her head, but as soon as she stopped convulsing, they forced her face back up and replaced the cloth again. Three more pitchers sat on the table.

Three more times they replaced the cloth. Three more times she gasped for breath. And then it was over. They were out of water.

The man who held her head undid her bonds and helped her off the table. Her legs shook, and she threw up all over him. He let go of her, and she fell to the floor. Sid forgot himself and tried to fly down to her, but Theo held tight.

I know this is hard, Theo said. *But she did it. Let her have the glory of this. Don't go rescuing her.*

Sid stilled. Theo was right. Aspen had to be very weak by now though. Sid didn't know how she was going to get through the last two tasks.

Almost immediately, Anasazi, the canyon dragon, stepped forward. Sid cringed.

He is going to probe her mind isn't he? Sid asked.

Yes.

That's not too bad. It's uncomfortable, but not life threatening. Sid was relieved. At least she wouldn't get hurt during this test.

It is different for a human.

Different how? The dread began again.

It is excruciatingly painful, and if she resists at all, she will die. He will probe every part of her mind, and she is not allowed to guard any part. If she does, his probing will kill her. This could be the end of her. She just withstood a possible drowning to protect a secret. If she doesn't allow him access to that secret, she'll die.

Sid tried to open his wings. Aspen would not allow her mind to be probed without resistance. He had to get down there before it began. Theo's tail was strong, and Obsidian was trapped. He tried to pull away, and the spikes on Theo's tail tore holes in Sid skin. He didn't register pain.

Obsidian, calm down! Theo screamed.

Sid didn't answer but continued pulling away. Everett's tail came up over his other side, and the strength surprised Sid. He continued to move backwards and forward to loosen their grips. It didn't work. Aspen was still lying on the ground. Her body convulsing.

Aspen, Sid yelled.

Anasazi looked up at him. *Stay out of this unless you want to bring about her death.*

Sid calmed and watched with horror. Anasazi was going to kill her. Sid would never be able to stare into those beautiful green eyes or run his fingers through her hair again. He wouldn't take her flying, and she wouldn't take him to play with the bears. She would never grow up and have children. Sid robbed her of her future. This was his fault. Why should she have to die because of him? It wasn't fair.

Anasazi stepped back. Aspen's body twitched.

Is she still alive?

Yes, she is. Will you stay here?

Yes

Everett and Theo let go. Sid stood up, the blood flowing down his underside. Everett sighed.

Hang on a moment. I'll call Sequoia.

Sequoia flew up and healed Sid's wounds. *I'm not the one who needs help. It's Aspen,* Sid said.

I'll take care of her when she has completed the test. She's only got one more. You picked a good one, Obsidian.

CHAPTER 36

ASPEN PULLED HERSELF up off the floor. Her head ached, and every breath was a challenge. Her legs shook, and her hair still reeked of vomit. But she was alive, thanks to Kairi, and there was only one task to go. The final dragon, a gigantic white one, stepped forward.

So you wish to be Obsidian's queen? the white dragon asked.

"Yes," Aspen replied. "Very much so."

I am Winerva, leader of the arctic dragons. I'm surprised you made it to me. However, you still have to pass my test. You will find that I am not quite as gentle as the others. There is little possibility of you dying during the actual test. However, if you fail, I will kill you. It is my right to do so.

Bring him in, she commanded to the small yellow dragons guarding the doors.

They opened the door, and in walked a golden dragon. He was magnificent. He approached Aspen and hung his head.

As queen you will find yourself in a position of handing out judgments to those that break the law. You must understand how to be fair, yet abide by our laws. The council acts as a court and decides whether or not a dragon is guilty of a crime. Your duty, along with the king, is to carry out all punishments.

Aspen studied the gold dragon while Winerva spoke. He had beautiful black eyes, and his wings sparkled, even in the darkness.

This dragon has been presented before the court and found guilty for killing several humans and one dragon. We decided that due to the horrific nature of his crimes that he be sentenced to death.

A large sword materialized on the floor at Aspen's feet.

Your task is to be his executioner. He will not fight back. This should be easy. The sword is sharp enough that it will cut of his head without too much effort.

Aspen stared at the sword. It the last thing she would have to endure to be with Sid forever. But how could she slay a dragon? Even if he had done those horrible things. It didn't seem right that she begin her reign by killing one. She hesitated but picked up the sword. It was lighter than she expected.

Perhaps, the white dragon said. *It would be beneficial for you to see him as one of your own.*

Aspen looked up at Sid, hoping he could give her some sort of hint as to what she was *supposed* to do. The look on his face was not comforting. He looked angry and tormented. Aspen turned, and a young man knelt at her feet.

Having him in human form was not going to be easier. How could she look him in the eye and cut off his head?

He looked up, and his face paled.

"What is your name?" Aspen asked.

"My name is Tendoy, and, Your Majesty, I beg you for mercy."

"Did you eat a human?"

He grasped the bottom of Aspen's pant leg and buried his face in her feet. "But it was by accident. I swear. I was going after a cow, and he was standing behind it. I never saw him, I promise."

"When did this happen?"

"Yesterday. It was an accident."

"What about all those humans before that."

"I had nothing to do with that."

She spun to face Winerva. "Is this true? Did he only eat a human as an accident?"

The tiny river dragon spoke. "He was presented before the council last evening and found guilty of all the human deaths."

"Did he admit it?"

"No, but that is irrelevant. There is not more than one dragon flying around eating humans. He made up that story when he got caught."

"How was he caught?"

"One of our guards saw him eat the human."

"Was there a cow?"

"Yes, but again, irrelevant. He's using that as an excuse. Your job, as Winerva pointed out, is not to judge but to ensure that the punishment is carried out."

Little girl, Winerva said, *you are taking too long. Kill him and be done with it.*

Aspen spun the sword in her hand and took three deep breaths. Then she swung the sword. At the last minute she stopped. This was not right.

"No," she said, throwing the sword down at his feet. "Killing him would be wrong. Especially considering we do not know for sure he is guilty. As queen it is also my privilege to change the sentence if I wish. I banish him from all contact. He will live out his days as a human. Food, shelter, and water will be provided. He will have no contact with either dragon or human."

Aspen looked at him. "If you fail to meet any of those conditions, your custodians will bring you back to me, and I will kill you. You will receive no more mercy from me. Now go, I wish to never to see your face again. When you die, we will leave your body to rot in your cage."

Aspen looked up and nodded to the two dragons guarding the door. She had no idea if she was doing the task correctly or not, but she would not have his blood on her hands. She hoped that afterwards she could figure out if he was really guilty or not. If he was not, she could bring him back out of isolation.

She once again thwarted the council's intentions. I'm not sure they know what to do with her, Everett said.

I'm convinced she will make a great queen, Sid replied.

Me too, but I'm afraid they may not think so. Winerva, especially. This task has always been the most difficult, and Winerva has never done the same one twice. Her tests always have had two possible outcomes. Either the woman carries out the task, or she proves her inability to do so. Aspen did not do either of these things. She showed mercy, yet followed through with the judgment. Winerva must be furious.

Can we go down there? Sid was so proud of Aspen. She never faltered, and she proved to many of the dragons that should could hold her own.

No, not yet, they have to announce their decision first.

Sid decided it was time to acknowledge Theo's presence. *Theo, I need you to take care of something for me.*

I thought you were going to kill me.

I was, but then I realized I wouldn't have anyone to do my dirty work for me if you were gone.

Smart choice, Your Majesty.

If you ever call me that again, I will kill you. I may be your king, but I am first and foremost your friend.

Okay, what do you need me to do?

Make sure Aspen's orders concerning Tendoy are carried out. Find a couple of canyon dragons to watch over him. They can watch his mind without actually having to be in his presence.

Got it, anything else?

Nope. But see if you can figure out if he really is guilty or not. Something doesn't feel right about this.

Theo left, and Sid felt better about the Tendoy situation. He sat down next to Everett. The old dragon was breathing rapidly. *How much longer?* Sid was getting tired of waiting.

Not long, I believe the holdup is whether or not she passed Winerva's test. They are calling for us. We should go.

Everett stumbled and got to his feet. His creaking wings opened. He took to the sky and fell several feet before his wings caught, and he glided to the floor. Sid wondered if Everett had the ability to make it home.

Sid soared down after him and landed. Aspen leaned up against him, the bright sword still in her hands. *You did great.*

If that's true, then what's taking them so long?

Winerva's upset because you didn't do what she wanted.

She's nasty, isn't she? How on earth was I supposed to kill a dragon?

She's intimidated by you. A dragon king's strength depends on the strength of his queen. You are unusually adept at being a dragon queen. That would make me a very forceful king. She would like nothing else than a weak king so the arctic dragons can take over again.

Aspen squeezed his neck, and they waited. The dragons were restless, and Sid could tell they were arguing. Suddenly, Winerva broke away from the group and stormed right for them.

She brought her large head in front of Aspen, who moved away from Sid.

You failed. She said so everyone could hear her.

She lifted her head up, opened her jaws wide. Aspen moved faster than Sid thought was possible. She ran right for Winerva and brought the sword up. Winerva's neck went right into it as her jaw slammed into the cave floor. Aspen moved around the dragon, dragging the sword along with her, beheading Winerva.

Sid flew to Aspen, and she dropped the sword. "I'm sorry. I didn't mean to kill her; I was just trying to stay alive."

I know.

Not a single dragon moved. Aspen hugged Sid's neck tightly. The sound of Aspen's rapid breathing filled Sid's ears. He watched the remaining council. Would they kill Aspen now after everything she'd been through? The stench of blood hung heavy in the air. Sid wanted to move away from the corpse, but he was afraid his movement might cause a shift in the silence, and they might attack.

They were talking. He could see it as each dragon shifted his eyes or snorted colored smoke. What would they do?

"Aspen, Obsidian, come here please," said Xanthous.

Sid moved forward slowly, Aspen leaning on his side. Her body trembled against his.

"We made our decision, though it was not unanimous. Throughout the testing, Aspen showed great strength and many other qualities that we admire in dragon queens. Winerva disagreed and tried to take matters into her own hands. You acted as any leader or queen would do and defended yourself."

Sid held his breath, unsure if he heard Xanthous correctly.

"Aspen," he said, "step forward please."

She walked toward him.

"You have passed. You will be the next dragon queen."

She sank to her knees and cried. Sid changed to his human form so he could comfort her properly. She sobbed in his arms.

"There are some conditions, however," Xanthous continued. "This is a highly unusual situation. Most dragon queens are in their thirties. We as a council decided it would be best if Obsidian finished his human experience. Because of this, we will not perform the bonding. You will wait until Sid has completed his training."

A bald eagle swept into the room.

"Valentine the fire dragon has turned black," the eagle screeched.

Sid's heart stopped. Everything in the room seemed to move in slow motion. Xanthous's mouth dropped open. Kairi's eyes widened. Sequoia let a small flame. After thousands of years, the Prophecy of the Three Dragon Kings was finally being fulfilled.

"Aspen we have to do this now!" Sid shouted.

"Do what?" she asked.

"The ceremony and the bonding," Sid said. She didn't get it. He knew she didn't, but he didn't have the time to be patient. If the prophecy was being fulfilled, that meant the war was coming, and he needed her strength. He couldn't do this without her.

"You mean get *married*?" she squeaked. Her eyes bugged. She crossed her arms and backed away from him. Sid rolled his eyes. She could stand up to Winerva, but the idea of marriage scared her.

"No," Sid explained. "But you must step forward and become the dragon queen. Dragons don't get married, but we do mate for life. We do not have to do *that* part right now. Dragon kings receive a great deal of power from their queens. That is why the queens go through the tests. A weak queen means a weak king. That ceremony plus the bonding will ensure that power."

She put her fingers on her temples and squeezed her eyebrows together. "But I don't understand. Ten minutes ago they said the ceremony could wait. Why does it have to be now?"

Sid grew frustrated. "I didn't tell you to do this. I never asked you to become queen. That is a choice you made. You came here today prepared to give your life, and you almost did. I'm sorry if the timing isn't right for you. Ten minutes ago the dragon community was at peace. In a very short time we will be at war, and I need all the strength I can get. I will explain this all later. Right now we must perform the ceremony." He walked over to Everett.

"We will do the ceremony now. Are you ready?"

Sid looked back and saw Aspen had not moved. She raised her eyebrows at him.

"No," she said.

"No what?" Sid asked.

"No, I will not do the ceremony, at least not until someone tells me what is going on."

Everett looked at her, his large gray eyes glistening.

Aspen, he said speaking to both of them. *Has Sid ever told you the story about the three dragon kings?*

"You mean the one where the three dragon kings defeat the white witch from the north?" she asked.

Yes, that one. It was a prophecy made during my youth. Three dragon kings will rise and defeat the dragon who sought to usurp power and enslave humanity. Never before has there been more than one dragon king. Today, an eagle came and declared that one more king has been found. A third will surely be discovered soon. There were many prophecies made during the time of my youth, many of them forgotten. He looked off into the distance.

The council closed in on them. Xanthous spoke.

"We did not think you would be unwilling to serve."

She stood up. "No, I'm willing. I just wanted to understand. We can do it now."

Sid grabbed her hand and pulled her close, his mind spinning. Another dragon king. That meant that his reign would be tainted by war and fear. At least he wouldn't have to go through it alone.

Xanthous approached Everett and touched his snout to the old dragon's head.

"Thank you, Xanthous," Everett said.

Everett placed himself before Aspen and Sid. "Obsidian, you have observed the testing of the queen, do you approve?"

"Yes," he replied.

"Very good, Obsidian, please wait next to me for the rest of the ceremony."

Sid looked at him, puzzled, but he moved next to Everett anyway. Since the timing of the ceremony was not expected, no one explained to Sid how this would go. He just had to sit and wait.

Dragon queen. Aspen was going to be the dragon queen. Her whole life she had chased after those gorgeous creatures, and now she would become a part of their society.

Everett continued talking. "You will receive gifts from each dragon. These abilities reflect their own gifts. By receiving these gifts, you will become very powerful, but it will take some time to get used to them. Following the gifting, I will complete the bonding."

Aspen was not sure what to do. She looked up at the dragons, and Sequoia came forward.

The woodland dragons have been given the gift of compassion and healing. Damien, the dragon you saw during your test, is one of our greatest failures. He will not allow our healers near him. I gift you with the ability to heal those around you, both physically and emotionally.

She touched the top of Aspen's head. She thanked her, and Sequoia moved back.

Nedra, the underground dragon, flew up and landed on Aspen's shoulder. *I have two gifts for you, but they are only useful in dire circumstances. You will have the ability to lift that which is beyond your strength as well as hide yourself from unfriendly eyes.* He placed he snout on her temple. She felt nothing, but was certain those gifts would be useful someday.

Eros then stepped up.

We fire dragons have been given the gift of passion and the power of fire. Without us, the flame of our fellow tribes would go out. To give the gift of fire to a human would be foolish; however, what I can give you is the gift to bear dragon children. Without it you would be barren. Dragon and human seed does not mix well.

He placed his great snout on her head, and Aspen could feel the heat.

Next Pearl stepped forward, smiling. *I suppose you already know what my gift is. Sid has surely interpreted your feelings on numerous occasions. I give you the gift to feel what others around you feel. Realize that this gift can be overwhelming.*

As Pearl pulled away, Aspen could immediately feel many different things, happiness, sorrow, and anger.

Xanthous approached her. Aspen smiled at him. He was one of her favorite dragons so far. That could be because he hadn't tried to torture her though. "Aspen, as you know, we river dragons have been gifted with the ability to speak. You already have that capability. So I give you the ability to communicate in all tongues, no matter what form they may take. This also gives you the ability to speak with others through your mind, including humans."

Aspen thanked him and tried not to think too hard about the ramifications of his gift.

When he stepped back, Kairi, the sea dragon, came forward. Aspen flinched.

I won't hurt you again. I hope you realize that what I did was necessary.

Aspen did not believe it, but she kept those thoughts to herself. *Can I ask you a question?*

Certainly.

How many queens have you tested?

Including you? Two.

Did you tell them the same secret?

Of course, I knew they would be good queens. I did not, however, tell the five potential queens who tested before them that particular secret.

What did you tell them?

Something trivial, I forget. Two of them couldn't keep the secret, and the other three died during Anasazi's father's test.

Thank you for trusting me. I would not have passed Anasazi's test without that secret.

You are welcome. Now it is time for me to give you a gift. The sea dragons have the ability to shield their minds from all dragons, including the canyon dragons. I give you the ability to keep your thoughts to yourself unless you're willing to give them.

This gift Aspen was very grateful for. She did not like her thoughts being open to everyone.

There were only two dragons left. Aspen was getting tired. Anasazi came to her. *I suppose my gift is obvious. I will not waste time with words.* He placed his great orange snout on the top of her head and then took his place back with the other dragons.

Aspen was bombarded with thoughts. It was dizzying. She tried to find Sid's and focus on those, but it was too difficult.

Exhaustion overwhelmed her. The gifts were too powerful. She wasn't sure she could handle anymore.

None of the dragons moved for a few moments. Aspen wasn't sure what was going on.

Everett, can you give her the gift? Sid asked.

It is not mine to give. We need to do the bonding, and then I have one last gift to give.

Everett, Sid begged. *Without longevity I will be weak, and she will die.* His grip tightened around her waist.

It looks like you will have to make do without it. I am not an arctic dragon. Therefore, I cannot give an arctic gift.

"Aspen, Sid, kneel in front of me facing each other. You must stay in the kneeling position, and you must be touching one another."

Sid raised his eyebrows at Aspen and scooted forward so his chest touched hers. She collapsed against him. She didn't care what they did as long as she got some sleep soon. She knew this was a big deal. It was akin to getting married, but she couldn't summon the excitement. Sid was buzzing with energy and had a goofy grin on his face.

He wrapped his arms around her in a hug, and she did the same. It was good to be close to him. She could see Everett out of the corner of her eye. He opened his mouth and a jet of white flame engulfed them. The flame was not hot, but it had an immediate effect. She could literally feel herself merging with Sid. She could hear his thoughts, feel his emotions, and fully understand him to the core. His memories became her memories. It was exhilarating.

Then as suddenly as it began, it ended.

Sid stood up and pulled her to her feet. "Are you alright?" he asked.

"No, but I will be. I'm really tired."

"Okay, as soon as Everett leaves, we'll go find a place to rest."

Everett wheezed behind them. "Obsidian, I need you to come here, in your dragon form."

Sid changed and approached Everett. Aspen sat on the ground and tried to keep her eyes open. She saw Everett and Sid talking to each other, and then sleep overtook her.

CHAPTER 37

SID WOKE ASPEN, and she climbed on his back. They flew out of the cavern and down a tunnel. Soon they landed in a large cave. Sid was sad, but she couldn't read his thoughts. He changed back into human form.

"Why are you upset?" Aspen asked.

"Everett's dead. I'm not sure I understand, and I don't really want to think about it."

Aspen's mind spun. She didn't know Everett, but everything that had happened in the last several hours had been so surreal. She couldn't even begin to comprehend the things going on around her.

Sid kissed her softly. "It's time for me to be a proper king again."

"What do you mean?"

"You reek."

Aspen slugged him.

"Ow, it's true."

"You still don't have to point it out." Aspen pouted and crossed her arms.

"I'm sorry. However, it's tradition for the king to take care of the queen after her test." He picked her up and carried her into another room.

Bright light reflected off the gemstone-studded walls. The whole place sparkled. In one corner there was an enormous four-poster mahogany bed with drapes around the entire thing. Along the far wall, a fire danced in large fireplace. A couch and two chairs stood before it. The room also contained three armoires, a table and chairs, and a large steaming pool.

Sid set her down next to the pool. It smelled like lilacs and roses. Everything she went through today was worth it for this alone. Sid tested the water with his fingers and then came back.

He stood in front of Aspen. "Arms up."

Aspen obeyed, not really thinking about what he said. He tugged at the corners of her t-shirt and then pulled it up over her head. "You know you are not getting laid tonight right? You told me this wasn't like getting married, so I am not obligated to have sex with you."

He grinned. "I know that. I'm not trying to 'get laid.'"

"So then why are you taking my clothes off?"

"Because you need a bath."

"I can take my clothes off myself."

"Not tonight you can't. Tonight it is my job to take care of you. This has been a tradition for thousands of years. Leave this one be."

"Fine." Aspen sighed and raised her hands up again as he pulled at her cami.

"Why on earth are you wearing more than one shirt?"

Aspen giggled as he stared at her bra.

"There is a clasp on the back. I'm sure you can figure it out."

He exhaled, moved around behind her, fiddled with the clasp for a few moments, and then slid her bra straps down her arms. She shivered as he ran his hands back up and then moved onto her jeans.

Aspen allowed him to finish undressing her. He stared at her. She felt suddenly self-conscious.

"You're gorgeous." He picked her up and carried her into the pool.

Sid didn't let Aspen do anything herself. It felt wonderful to have someone else to wash her hair and dress her. The nightgown he put on her was bright red with thin straps. She loved it.

He put her in bed and lay down beside her. He kissed her once more, and she fell into a glorious slumber.

The next morning Aspen woke feeling giddy. She knew at once that the feeling did not come from her. She rolled over, and Sid was sitting cross-legged on the bed.

"Hey gorgeous, did you sleep well?"

"Yeah, I don't even feel sore. What are you so happy about?"

"You and us." He beamed.

"How come I can't hear your thoughts?" Aspen asked.

He cocked his head to the side and moved her hair out of her eyes. "When Everett bonded us, I also gained your shield gift that you received from Kairi. We can both read almost anyone's thoughts but each other. We should visit Anasazi today though to learn how to control his gift. It would be annoying to have everyone's thoughts in our heads all time."

"Then what?"

"What do you mean?"

"What do we do then? There was a great deal of urgency to get all of this over with yesterday."

"The council and I discussed this last night after you fell asleep. You and I are going back to our lives as humans. We will pretend this hasn't happened yet."

Aspen was thoroughly confused. "Why?"

"The news of two new dragon kings is going to turn the dragon world into chaos. Very few of us know about the additional dragon kings yet, so we are taking actions but are keeping it secret. If suddenly

I am flying around, dragons are going to get suspicious. They know that I am supposed to be human for the next ten years."

"So what exactly are you all doing?"

"Pearl, Anasazi, and Kairi went north to smooth things over with the arctic dragons. Winerva was their leader. The arctic dragons will be very angry. I expect your killing her will speed things along with the prophecy. Eros and Theo have gone to take care of Valentine. Finding a queen for him is crucial. With the war coming, we'll need all three kings at their top strength. That can't happen without queens. Theo's going to bring him back here, and we'll help him."

"Do you know Valentine?"

Sid smiled. "I've never met him, but he's Damien's son. It's another reason I pushed for training him here instead of in his home in Hawaii. Damien doesn't know yet."

Aspen swelled with happiness. She was very fond of Damien, and she was glad he would finally get the opportunity to see his son again.

"What about the third dragon king?"

"Xanthous and Sequoia are in search of him. He could be anywhere. Until these things are done, there isn't much we can do. For now, there is peace. Enjoy it while you can."

"What about Skye?"

"She'll stay with us. Rumors were already floating around the dragon world that I was misbehaving and she had to come put me in line. It is better for her to stay. Plus, in spite of Skye being a sea dragon, she's not very good at keeping secrets. We need to keep her close."

"Except when she dropped me off, she said she was going to stay with her parents. We might not find her."

"She'll come back when she finds out we're both still alive."

"Can we tell my parents? They deserve to know. Rowan already knows."

"It probably is best that we tell them. As queen you may have to take a few trips with me, and you'll be expected to make decisions with me. The only reason we did not consult with you on the decisions we made last night was because you were dead to the world. Your parents are going to have to accept that you are no longer just a teenager in high school. You'll also have to prepare them for the time when you will no longer be part of this world."

Aspen's stomach tensed at that thought. She'd forgotten the promises she made when she agreed to be the dragon queen. At least, with Sid staying human for a while, she'd be able to see them for a little while longer.

Aspen laid a hand on Sid's chest. "What about all these? Wasn't the point that you were creating your own council? They've got to be angry about that."

Sid sighed. "They are. I thought about getting Helios to finish the job. It would be the safest thing to do. But it's not the most diplomatic. By allowing the current council to remain in power, I will have more dragons on my side when the war does break out."

They got ready and spent a few hours with Anasazi's mate. She showed them how to open their minds up when they wanted to. Sid turned back into his dragon form, and they flew toward home. Aspen was nervous about telling her parents. They were usually pretty open minded, but explaining that she was now a queen would be difficult.

Aspen opened the door to her house, Sid on her heels laughing and carrying on. They walked into the kitchen and dark feelings filled Aspen's chest. Fear, anxiety, and grief. Her mother sat at a table clutching a coffee mug. Mom looked up, paused for a moment, then ran to her. She crushed Aspen in a hug.

"Oh, you're okay. Thank the stars."

"Mom, I'm fine. What's up?"

"We went to Sid's house yesterday looking for you, and no one was there. We've tried reaching you on the phone, and you wouldn't answer. No one had seen you. Where have you been? I thought for sure you'd both been taken. Another ranger was killed yesterday. We've been worried sick."

Stacey paused and looked around the room. "Where is Rowan?"

"He's not here?"

"No, your car was found on the side of the road, but no one was there. We thought the dragon got all three of you."

"But then where's Rowan?"

EPILOGUE

A FEW MILES AWAY on the top of a snow-capped mountain, a golden dragon bowed to large white one.

"You've done well. Especially throwing the blame on Tendoy like that," the white dragon said.

"No one suspected me. It was easy really. He had been careless."

"Winerva would have been proud."

"I'm sorry I didn't protect her. I had already left by the time Aspen killed her."

"I know. But my aunt expected it. She left me ready to take her place. Once Obsidian and Aspen are dead, we'll be prepared to take over the council. And then you, Prometheus, and I will rule as king and queen," said Candide.

THE END

FROM THE AUTHOR

I HOPED YOU ENJOYED reading Aspen. If you are interested in the next book in the series, it will be released in July 2016 and can be purchased here:

KimberlyLoth.com/valentine

Want to a free book? Click here to get the first book of my other series, *The Thorn Chronicles* absolutely free:

KimberlyLoth.com

If you enjoyed this book, or even if you didn't, please consider leaving a review. As an Indie author, reviews are crucial.

Thank you for reading!

ABOUT THE AUTHOR

KIMBERLY LOTH CAN'T decide where she wants to settle down. She's lived in Michigan, Illinois, Missouri, Utah, California, Oregon, and South Carolina. She finally decided to make the leap and leave the U.S. behind for a few years. She spent two wild years in Cairo, Egypt. Currently, she lives in Shenzhen, China with her husband and two kids. She is a middle school math teacher by day (please don't hold that against her) and YA author by night. She loves romantic movies, chocolate, roses, and crazy adventures. *Aspen* is her seventh novel.

ACKNOWLEDGEMENTS

THESE GET HARDER and harder to write the more books I publish, because I'm terrified I'm going to forget someone.

Thanks go first to my amazing publicist and best friend, Virginia. She does so much. I don't know what I'd do without her.

Big thank you to Will, Xandi, and AJ. I know I've been super busy with book stuff lately and I'm so, so grateful for your support and belief in me.

Mandy, Kristin, and Karen. You three are my writing tribe. Thank for the unending emails and support.

To my team, Kelley, Suzi, Rebecca, and Colleen. It takes a village to publish a book. Thanks for your amazing talent in taking my manuscript and turning it into a book.

Brittany, thanks for the proofread. My eyes don't see those things you do!

Finally, a huge thank you to my fans. Especially those superfans (you know who you are). You all are amazing and I love hearing from you. Thanks for your support and spreading the word.

CPSIA information can be obtained
at www.ICGtesting.com
Printed in the USA
LVHW01s1532100518
576716LV00003B/748/P